She Was What Clayton Wanted.

And he'd see to it that he was what she wanted. It was simple. He smiled at her.

"Why are you smiling?"

"I was thinking about kissing you."

"Clayton!" She pretended to be scandalized.

He knew she wasn't. Her cheeks pinked nicely, but it was because she was pleased he was teasing her.

"Your hair's so pretty."

"You're embarrassing me." She put the back of her hand under the side of her hair and pushed it back a little.

He smiled because it was so easy to lure a woman. He'd have her soon, then she'd know about him, how it would be with him, and she'd love him. It wouldn't take any tricks at all. He would just be himself, and she'd fall right into his trap.

Dear Reader:

Welcome to the world of Silhouette Desire. Join me as we travel to a land of incredible passion and tantalizing romance—a place where dreams can, and do, come true.

When I read a Silhouette Desire, I sometimes feel as if I'm going on a little vacation. I can relax, put my feet up and become transported to a new world ... a world that has, naturally, a perfect hero just waiting to whisk me away! These are stories to remember, containing moments to treasure.

Silhouette Desire novels are romantic love stories—sensuous yet emotional. As a reader, you not only see the hero and heroine fall in love, you also feel what they're feeling.

In upcoming books look for some of your favorite Silhouette Desire authors: Joan Hohl, BJ James, Linda Lael Miller and Diana Palmer.

So enjoy!

Lucia Macro
Senior Editor

LASS SMALL

THE LONER

SILHOUETTE *Desire*

Published by Silhouette Books New York

America's Publisher of Contemporary Romance

SILHOUETTE BOOKS
300 East 42nd St., New York, N.Y. 10017

ISBN: 0-373-05594-3

First Silhouette Books printing September 1990

Books by Lass Small

Silhouette Romance

An Irritating Man #444
Snow Bird #521

Silhouette Desire

Tangled Web #241
To Meet Again #322
Stolen Day #341
Possibles #356
Intrusive Man #373
To Love Again #397
Blindman's Bluff #413
Goldilocks and the Behr #437
Hide and Seek #453
Red Rover #491
Odd Man Out #505
Tagged #534
Contact #548
Wrong Address, Right Place #569
Not Easy #578
The Loner #594

Silhouette Books

Silhouette Christmas Stories 1989
"The Voice of the Turtles"

LASS SMALL

finds that living on this planet at this time is a fascinating experience. People are amazing. She thinks that to be a teller of tales of people, places and things is absolutely marvelous.

One

It was August that year when the fires began to get really bad; and like the other creatures, Clayton Masterson moved down from the mountains west above Yellowstone.

Before Clayton left his place, he had carried the irreplacables such as his parents' picture and their family Bible out to the root cellar. Then he'd dragged out the necessaries, including his mattress, the quilts, the chain saw, the television and its dish, the traps, guns, pots and pans. He added those in the root cellar that his great-great granddad had blasted into dead rock. Then Clayton had closed the wooden door and covered it with dirt.

There wasn't much real dirt where Clayton lived in the eastern part of the Rocky Mountains. On the ground in his woods, there were pine needles and rotting leaves, but he cleared away the decaying limbs and trees. All that was tinder for fires.

Long ago he had carried back dirt from the meadows to spread a thick layer on the almost flat roof of his low-built cabin, and he kept the covering clean of debris. His dad had said, "Keep your weapons, tools and your roof clean. Keep your blades sharp." Those were rules of survival.

His mother had said, "Be tidy. Keep your place neat. Inside and out. And yourself, too."

And his dad had cautioned, "Rub yourself with grasses if you go hunting. Animals can smell coffee, tobacco, onions and soap."

Clayton had listened. He hadn't allowed the accumulation of undergrowth to keep a fire burning overly long, so the cabin should be okay, unless the wild winds rushed the flames into a fire storm. Nothing could survive that.

Clayton took a last look around. The land had been a Masterson holding since the late 1700s. If the threatening fire did go through, the rock and dirt would probably protect his cache in the contrived cave. Clayton knew that he would rebuild the cabin, just as his ancestors had had to do a time or two. This was his home, his place in the world. He would return when the fires were controlled.

Into a backpack, Clayton then put some pemmican and granola from his mother's particular blend of ingredients. He added a change of clothing, a rolled blanket and his carefully wrapped fiddle. Then he took down his rifle. He was ready. He whistled for Wolf and put the wide, yellow collar on him. It would identify the wolf as a pet. After that, they began their descent.

In such a remote place, Clayton never saw anyone unless he needed something from town. As self-sufficient as he was, it was rare that he ventured down into "civilization." He didn't do that often because he was awkward with people. He didn't fit.

But he'd been trained by his parents in his share of responsibility. The men in his family had been in every war this country had ever fought, and while his mother had been a flower child, his dad had served in Vietnam. "Everyone has to help, even if it's disagreeing with what's going on," they'd told Clayton. "It's our country. We can't just sit around and not do our share."

That was why— But he still couldn't let his mind even touch on that.

So it was because of his parents' conviction about one being a part of the whole, that Clayton had trained as a smoke jumper the year before. As they had been, he was a volunteer fire watcher. Most of the mountain people were. Clayton had a radio to report anything suspicious to the rangers whose headquarters were some distance east of him.

As he went out, Clayton trudged past a ranger in the fire tower several peaks away from his place. They'd never spoken. Clayton hadn't wanted to intrude on the man. But Clayton's Wolf knew the man kept a bitch dog. She'd always come out on the porch-like walk to stand next to the ranger, to look over at Wolf and wag her tail. Wolf had stared back.

The man was lonely there. He'd lugged the dog all the way up that ladder.

After a time, Clayton reached the town of Gasp. It had been named for the last gasp of breath it had taken to get there. The residents numbered all of thirty-some odd, and the two-lane highway was the only road in town. There was a filling station, a general store, a café for travelers, and beyond those buildings were several houses.

Clayton soon realized Gasp was deserted. Before, there'd always been somebody loose in the town who'd lift a recognizing hand, and Clayton was surprised he missed the greeting. That meant he'd anticipated it. Without it, he felt . . . almost abandoned. For a loner, that was an odd feeling.

So why should he feel as if the world had gone off and left him? He stood in the empty town and looked around. How could it seem so lonely when the un-peopled woods didn't?

Clayton was almost thirty. Strong. Big-shouldered. Wide-chested. Male. His hair was dark and his eyes green. He'd worn a beard ever since he'd tangled with a cougar whose claws had ripped his face. The beard didn't cover all the claw marks, but those that showed were neat. On TV, not too many city men wore beards; therefore Clayton had the feeling that women didn't like hairy men.

Women wanted men who looked good. Well, maybe not all women. He knew a man over a couple of peaks who was the ugliest, dirtiest creature Clayton had ever seen. Although the man was even *called* Stinky, he'd gotten a mail-order bride. A woman had advertised for a man, and old Stinky had shown up at Clayton's place and said, "I hear you can write nice."

Clayton admitted to that talent.

"I need a letter for this here woman," Stinky explained. "Will you do that for me? I'll give you that skin."

The lynx pelt was a beauty. "That's not legal."

"This one was hit by a car and it's spine was busted. I got an okay for it."

So Clayton wrote the letter, but he did it outside, sitting on the stoop, upwind from the man.

It had been a year or so before he came across Stinky with a woman who was carrying a load on her back. Stinky had said to the woman, "That's him. He wrote that letter."

The gap-toothed woman had grinned at Clayton. The mail-order bride was a strong, coarse woman who pleased her husband. But she was so different from Clayton's mother, that he'd since been leery of the advertisements for marriages.

Clayton was an innocent, but he'd watched television. He'd seen men with women, and watching them, Clayton would feel his body become restless and needy. But he didn't know how to make contact with a woman. In the town below his mountains there were some women who had looked at him, but he figured they were scornful of a man who was the way he was, off in the mountains and alone. He didn't know how to explain himself to them or even how to begin a conversation.

As he and Wolf had walked down his mountain, they'd seen two bucks over a way. Their fighting was not yet serious, but they practiced for the combat that would come with the beginning of the rutting season. Wolf wasn't hungry and ignored the two animals, but Clayton understood them and their building mating need. His own need was all-year-long, and during winter nights and the long days of summer, he paced restlessly, impatient in his solitude.

He wondered if he'd ever know a woman. Ever feel her hands on him or be allowed to put his on her. Who could she be? Who could be the woman who could love him?

In his mind he'd never seen the elusive woman of his dreams. No face came clear to his imagination, but she must be somewhere in the world. And in the depths of lonely nights, he'd begun to believe that he would have to find her. The escalating forest fires were a good excuse to begin the search.

The town of Gasp had never known locked doors. If anyone wanted to come inside, they would, so why tempt somebody to break a window or ruin a door? Clayton went into the silent, empty general store and looked around. He didn't need anything.

Drawn to it, he moved slowly over to the rack holding several pretty women's dresses. And he looked at them. Since no one was there, he realized he could touch them without seeming strange. And he did that. Then he went to the drawers behind the counter. He slowly opened them until he found the women's slips and underwear. The filmy garments were all in one drawer. Gently he put his hands on the silken wisps and smiled a little and shook his head once at the thought of anyone wearing something so nothing.

Think what it would be for a man to give a woman something like that and . . . and to see her wear it for him.

The sound of an approaching truck suddenly came to his hearing, and Clayton slammed the drawer shut, ran outside and waved the truck down. A man looked at him cautiously. Clayton asked, "You going to the fires?"

"Yeah."

"Can I ride along?"

"In back."

Clayton understood. The man didn't want him or the wolf in the cab. The man wasn't sure of a stranger and he didn't know to trust him. Clayton smiled and said, "Obliged." He touched the surface of the stacked truck cargo, and Wolf hesitated a fraction, then jumped up effortlessly. Clayton got his pack and slung it and himself over onto the crowded truck bed. Then he had to arrange a few things so that he and Wolf would fit.

The wolf made an inquiring sound.

"It's okay." Clayton pulled the wolf close, then tapped on the window as a signal that he was ready. He settled his well-used Stetson firmly on his head, and the pickup sped away from Gasp.

Wolf was appalled. He struggled briefly with iron muscles opposing Clayton's own strength, but the man soothed the animal, his talk soft and reassuring. It took a while for Wolf to pull his head from under Clayton's arm and test the reality of that weird way of moving.

They rode a long way. Jackson was the only other place Clayton had ever been beyond Gasp. Now he watched the long road go by, and he felt like a traveler. The countryside stretched out and it was beautiful. He could see more from the truck because he didn't have to watch around him.

He felt that he was starting an adventure that could change his life. He was exhilarated. He rubbed Wolf's coat and laughed out loud, and the wolf silently laughed with him.

Eventually they drove to a meadow where a camp had been established along a road for the volunteers. Clayton thanked the man for the ride and got his wolf and gear from the truck. The man drove on. Clayton turned and walked carefully into the crowded field where volunteers were being organized...and *there she was!*

In all that movement, it was she whom he saw. The world slowed down and every sound, every shadow became important. She was his dream. She was perfect. He stared, his lips parted slightly as they did in a hunt so that his excited breath didn't betray him.

He watched her move, and she was like music. He saw her form, and it was ethereal. He wanted to go to her and kneel before her like the Knights of Old. But men didn't do that sort of thing on television. On TV they went over to the women, smiled confidently and said clever things.

Clayton's soul groaned in despair. How could he win her? He didn't have the glib tongue to call her interest to himself. So he watched from a distance. Hopelessly. If she ignored those clever-tongued men, how could Clayton Masterson ever catch her attention?

The laughing, teasing men said her name. They called her Shelley. She paid them no mind but busily laid out sandwiches and fruit. She was perfect. Her hair was long and blond and ruffled by the wind. Her eyes were gray—

"You volunteering?"

Some crass male voice interrupted Clayton's dream. He frowned a little and looked at the man who was tired, rugged and impatient. Clayton replied, "Yeah."

"Any experience?"

"Yeah."

"Go over to that truck," the man instructed. "You'll be issued equipment and gear. Report to that man by the table over there. That your dog? It's a wolf!"

"He's okay," Clayton soothed. "He does as I tell him."

"What'll he do while you're working? You can be days away."

"No worry there," Clayton explained. "He'll go along or he'll stay where I tell him."

"You should have left him at home."

Clayton shrugged. "I couldn't."

"What experience d'you have?"

"Trained last year as a fire jumper." Clayton watched the man's eyes flare with interest.

"Great! We can use you."

Although Clayton thought he'd be sent out immediately, the group had a couple of days for orientation and instruction. Each volunteer was issued protective clothing and told how to wear it and how to keep himself whole. They were given tools and shown how to use them. They were told to pay attention, not to get separated from their group and what to do if they did get separated. They were responsible for each other.

There weren't too many greenhorns, but they all listened. Some of the volunteers were women. And some of the men were uneasy that women would be involved on the fire line. They weren't sure that women could handle such a tough job.

The volunteers were shown maps and told about the fires. Their instructor was named Spears and he explained, "Up here, this is the fourth year of the worst drought in the history of this country. Although the trees are green and there is sap tar, there's no moisture. Last spring the twigs and grasses were down to twenty- or thirty-percent moisture. Generally it's eighty-percent. With last spring's heat wave and only half the rainfall, we're in trouble. Bush can survive one year of drought, but the second year it's bad and now it's a disaster waiting to happen."

Spears shifted his feet and went on earnestly, "We've come into a lot of criticism because we've allowed the lightning-started fires to burn. We used to fight them all, but after almost a hundred years of that, the forest preserves are tinder-boxes of dried windfalls and piled undergrowth just waiting for a spark. We're paying now for interfering with the natural fires.

"We're almost solely involved with trying to prevent the fires from overrunning habitations and towns. We'll be clearing firebreaks around populated places. Like any fire fighter, you're here to save houses and towns. It's going to be a long, hard job. Pray for cool weather and rain.

"Thank you for volunteering. I know you're impatient to begin, but we need to be sure you all know what you're supposed to do. So we'll train those who are new, and we'll refresh the skills of those who've been away from forest and brush fires.

"We believe we'll have a very hard month or two ahead of us...the rest of August and into September. Rest when you can, eat when you can, and sleep when you have the opportunity. There'll be portable showers. Keep clean when you can, and pay attention to any cuts or blisters. We have a good first-aid crew. Any questions?"

There were always questions. But this time, there was none.

Clayton saw that Shelley helped with putting out the food brought by truck to the group at mealtime. Clayton got to walk over and get in line so he was closer and got to really look at her. She had no flaws. She seemed unknowing of his attention. Concentrating on restocking the sandwiches and the milk and coffee, she worked with agility. She didn't even glance at him.

Clayton took his paper plate back to his pack and lounged there with studied casualness. She would never guess that he watched her. He was subtle.

And Wolf watched her.

Because Clayton's eyes never left her, he'd witnessed her first startled glimpse of Wolf. She questioned the man in charge of that group. His name was...Spears. Yes. Tom Spears. Spears replied to Shelley with gestures and touched his own throat, so Clayton knew he was explaining about the collar Wolf wore.

After supper was finished, Shelley talked to the wolf. When no one else was around her, the wolf was nearer to her. Clayton anguished over the fact that the wolf could be so obvious in his interest, while *he* had to stay back and pretend to look elsewhere. But Clayton had glanced around and seen that there were others who weren't as subtle as he, and in his mind just about all the men watched Shelley.

Clayton saw when she gave Wolf the first bit of tuna. She held it out and coaxed, but the wolf wouldn't approach, so she tossed it to the animal. He watched the tidbit alertly and saw where it fell, but he didn't go to it. After a minute the wolf turned his head and looked at his master. Clayton signaled. The wolf stood, went to the tuna and sniffed cautiously, then

checked again with his master. Clayton signaled again.
And the wolf carefully picked it up in his mouth and
went to Clayton, who gave the animal permission to
eat.

He thereby gave Shelley shared control over the
wolf.

Clayton glanced up to convey that fact, but Shelley
had gone on about her duties, and so Clayton was denied showing her who was master of the wolf. Well,
they'd have another day or so. He wondered if he
could use the wolf as a reason to speak to Shelley. On
TV, he'd seen men do that with dogs. Generally it had
been the woman's dog and a cute little one. Would a
wolf be any substitute? What would he say to her? He
had no idea.

He watched as some of the people organized a game
of baseball. Clayton had never played the game. The
players were lively and there was a lot of yelling. Pre-
dictably it was male against female. And the men were
indulgent. Then they had to work to win.

Clayton took his fiddle out of its wrappings and
carried it off, followed by Wolf. At a distance, the man
sat down, considered what his soul needed and began
to play. The wolf went off a way, lay down, put his
head on his paws and watched Clayton entertain him.
He was at that distance in order to protect the man.
There, the wolf could hear any sound that was wrong.

So the wolf knew when the people began to come
along and stand listening. Clayton was so involved
with the music that he wasn't aware. The wolf realized it was that way, had understood that early in their
relationship and had learned to take care of him in
those circumstances.

Clayton played with his soul. He always did. The fiddle was from his great-great grandfather, and the songs and melodies were forgotten ones his kinsmen had been taught. The tunes had been passed down through the years, and Clayton had learned them from his grandfather.

There in the woods, Clayton now played as the Spanish do beneath a balcony, to serenade his love. Shelley. Out of earshot, away from her, Clayton played for Shelley.

Was his music good enough to give to her? Would she accept that he'd never played for another woman? He hadn't even played his music for another soul. Not since his mother and father—but he couldn't remember that now.

He began to play the dances, the joyous gathering dances played in cabins all those years ago. Some sounded familiar to the delighted ears around, but they'd been changed a little. The rhythm was there, the toe-tapping lure.

His bow slid and the strings sang and the sound was flung through the trees, just as it had all those years past, making the air vibrate with the mark of something that wasn't there before. It was man leaving his mark. Another man; another mark. And the fiddle went gaily on, the notes slurred and wicked, and quick and funny.

As always when Clayton played, it was healing to his spirit. Playing had been important at many times in his life. And that was the first time in a long while that he'd played the happy songs that sang in his blood. He played for Shelley. Shelley. Was she named for the poet? He brought the song to its end with a flourish. And he paused. He would compose a song for—

There was a rush of applause! It sounded like wind through brittle leaves, but there were whistles and shouts and calls for "More!"

Clayton jerked around, looking startled. Then he laughed back at their laughter, got up, and he bowed!

"Encore!" "Bravo!" were the shouts, and again, "More! More!"

So he walked a pace of two, thinking, then he shouted, "Grab your partner, do-si-do, swing your lady, here we go! Who can call it?"

He didn't know the calls. He only knew the music. But one woman was a caller, and they began to dance. Only a few, tentatively, then they included others and finally there were several sets. There were men who sashayed, as men do when they think they're mimicking or imitating women, and they partnered other men. There were laughter and shouts and show-offs, and it was fun.

And Shelley danced. Everyone there wanted to dance with Shelley, and Clayton had trouble keeping the music light and airy. His jealousy burned in him. He was ashamed of the degrading emotion, but only in a tiny corner of his conscience. All the rest of him was steeped in jealousy.

After an hour's dancing, Clayton brought his music to a close with a flourish and again bowed to applause. "More," they begged. But he smiled and shook his head. "More!" they coaxed, but he said, "Another time."

That was what his mother used to say when he was little and wanted one more story. He wondered what she would think of Shelley.

Clayton saw her go over and lean down to the wolf. After a quick glance at Clayton to be sure his slave was

all right, the wolf sat up like a gentleman and contemplated the woman with interest. She held out the
back of her hand for him to sniff, and he was courteous about it. Her voice was soft as she said soothing
things to him, and he allowed her to touch his head,
his eyes again on his slave.

Clayton longed to be a wolf.

Before he could go over to them, he was blocked by
strangers who felt they now knew him and were free to
ask him questions. They made impulsive comments
that demanded a reply. "Where did you learn to play
like that?" one asked.

"My grandfather."

"I don't recognize most of the pieces," another
said. "Are they yours?"

"No, they've come down in my family. My people
have lived out here for a long time."

"No wonder you're a fire fighter," still another
commented. "This country must all seem like it's
yours."

"Yes."

And they teased him, "We'll help you save it."

His tongue didn't know how to reply to their teasing so he smiled. But when he looked up, Wolf was
alone. She had gone?

As others commented, one said, "That's not a violin. It's a real fiddle."

"It's been in my family for a long, long time."

"Beautiful." A small redhead breathed as she stood
in front of him, looking at Clayton.

He blushed and couldn't speak. Here was an op-
portunity to practice, and his tongue wouldn't work.
That was because he wasn't giving it anything to say.
It was his brain that was paralyzed; his tongue had to

have directions. He smiled down at the redhead. She grinned back and went off. His smile had been enough.

And he remembered how the bitch stood on the watchtower and smiled at Wolf, and the wolf had only looked. Maybe men didn't have to be glib. Maybe he just had to be interested?

He was in the group going back to the camp. He wasn't just along, he was a *part* of it. People made comments to him. It was very nice.

Since so many of the volunteers had young appetites, they all were fed a bedtime snack. Spears called, "Lights out in half an hour. Eat and—"

"Wash your te-e-e-eth," came a high-pitched, mocking male voice.

There were laughs.

Spears said, "Thank you for reminding us. Hit the sacks and sleep. No talking. You'll need the stored rest. Good night. Thanks for the music, Masterson."

Clayton blushed as he grinned in painful pleasure at being singled out. He stood in line with the others, and they moved aside saying he could be first since he'd played so hard. He was annoyed that they'd allow him to do that, because he wanted to stand and look at Shelley while the others selected their rolls and drink. He still didn't know how to reply easily, and studied how to act. His mouth smiled and that did seem to be enough.

But he was the first to leave the table. He didn't know how to stand around, eating, so he took the rolls and milk and went to his bedroll. Because of Wolf, he'd placed his bedroll a little separate from the others. He sat down and shared the gooey confection with the wolf who ate it. "It's not good for you," he whispered to the wolf.

But the wolf only ran his tongue over his teeth and smiled.

"If you were a real help, you'd go over there and bring her back here to my bedroll."

The wolf looked over to where Shelly was putting out the rest of the rolls.

Yet again, the wolf had seemed to understand Clayton's words. Clayton scoffed. What could a wolf know about men and women together? Then he remembered the bitch on the tower. How was he so different from a wolf?

So in his bedroll, he dreamed of Shelley. He dug his fingers into the wolf's scruff and dreamed it was Shelley's thick hair and murmured in his sleep. She turned and licked his nose, and the dreaming Clayton was startled that Shelley's tongue was so long and rough.

Two

___

Wakened by the first sounds of stirring the next morning, Clayton found Wolf was gone. With such a change in the animal's life, Clayton wondered if the wolf had reverted, if he'd heard the Call of the Wild. Clayton had automatically curled up onto an elbow to look for Shelley, and found her instantly. The wolf was over at the food truck smiling up at Shelley, who was bent over, talking to the damned pushy beast. But the animal was a connoisseur. Of the women at the meadow, Wolf had chosen the prime one.

She got a spoon and a pan, hitting them and calling, "Come and get it."

There was a generator truck, and the food was hot. Cereal, pancakes, toast, scrambled eggs with link sausages. Coffee and milk. There was tea for the peculiar ones and more sweet rolls.

In the crisp morning air they all breathed deeply and found the world was good. They ate too much, their appetites were ravenous, and their bodies sleepily comfortable. They smiled a lot and talk began. They were becoming acquainted.

Clayton stood in line and even let people in ahead of him until he could get his nerve up. Others spoke to Her and finally he managed a mumbled, "Good morning, Shelley."

She didn't hear him the first time so he cleared his throat and at the last possible minute as he was nudged along, he said again, "Good morning, Shelley."

And she gave him a quick smile.

That she did so with automatic reflex was plain to Clayton, but he was paralyzed that she had actually appeared to look at him. He took his plate over to his bedroll and sat there absently. The wolf got all the eggs and some of the sausages. He was being corrupted.

Then the wolf went around, smiling at others with real timidness. He collected a little egg over there, and caught midair some sausage tossed to him at another place, until he got back to Shelley who gave the animal part of a sweet roll. He was turning into a panhandler.

Then Wolf lay on the grasses, rolled onto his back and looked like a degenerate. Shelley leaned down and scratched the wolf's belly, and across the way Clayton groaned with envy.

While the crew showered, their bedrolls were hung on lines, then rolled up and stored in a truck for the day. The crew dressed in their issued gear. And Clayton found they would return to the same meadow that evening. He told Wolf to stay.

The crews were taken by school bus and put to work clearing firebreaks. It was to practice, but the lanes might be crucial if the rains didn't come or if the winds shifted. They were admonished again and again, "Where is your partner?... How many of you are there?... Is anyone missing?"

Sandwiches were brought to them at noon, and they sprawled around during the break and rested. When Spears felt they were ready, they would relieve one of the other crews already on the fire lines. They were like reserve troops in any battle.

They worked with a coffee break in the middle of the August afternoon, and were bused back to their meadow late in the day.

Wolf watched as the crew got out of the buses. He went to Clayton, who rubbed the wolf's head as he looked for Shelley.

They were all tired. Some of their muscles weren't used to such sustained work, and they weren't as lively as they'd been the night before. They showered in the trucks and put on clean clothes. They ate the hot meal that was waiting for them, and they dragged off to their bedrolls early.

Someone called, "Hey, Clayton? How about a little soothing music?"

Not aware that he didn't reply, Clayton got out his fiddle and plucked the strings to be sure it was in tune. Then he played the old songs: "Eating Goober Peas," "Shenandoah," songs from the War Between the States.

It was surprising how many knew the words. There were good voices that took up harmony, and there were some flat ones, pulled along fairly well, that enjoyed singing in a partly concealing group.

The music sounded very nice in that isolated place, and Clayton was filled with something emotional because he was a part of it. Instinct made him stop before the music was too much, too long, and they all slept deeply that night, although in the morning there were women who complained about the snoring.

So when Shelley banged the pan and called to them, "Come and get it," there was reluctance and groaning as they slowly removed themselves from the bedrolls.

Wolf went along with Clayton and stretched his nose up to sniff the table. Clayton cautioned the wolf, who gave his slave a chiding glance. Shelley laughed, for she had seen, and she made up a plate and set it in the grass for the wolf who... wolfed it down.

She smiled a quick, impersonal look at the wolf's owner, and Clayton blushed with exquisite pleasure. From his bedroll, Clayton noted when the wolf had licked the plate clean, and he gave the short whistle to bring the animal to him. Wolf gave the plate another lick before obeying.

Clayton had no other reason to call the wolf than to show Shelley that the animal was his. It had been done solely to call her attention to himself. She was busy. She didn't notice. She hadn't heard the too-loud whistle nor had she noted that the wolf had finished the plate and had been summoned.

Wolf came to Clayton and, with a glance, inquired the reason for his slave's whistle. There was none. Clayton offered the wolf some of the egg, but the animal wasn't interested. However he did indicate that he could manage a bit of pancake for old time's sake.

Clayton fed the wolf the bit and said, "You're being ruined."

Wolf licked his lips and smiled.

"I do understand, you know. I would do anything to have her attention."

The wolf looked over to Shelley.

"So you know when I'm talking about her?"

Wolf looked back at him.

"You do. Then go over and tell her that I'm the best man she could ever find, and that I want her to scratch my belly the same way she did yours yesterday."

Wolf loped off toward Shelley! All Clayton could think was: Thank God Wolf couldn't actually talk. But Clayton watched with some unease as to just what the wolf would do.

He went to Shelley, grinned and wagged his tail. Shelley laughed that delicious sound that was like fingers down a man's insides, and she leaned over and rubbed the wolf's head.

Clayton wished for a tail to wag, he was better than a wolf. He was a man. The man for Shelley.

The wolf trotted back, stopped by Clayton, sat down and watched his slave.

Clayton was taken aback. It was exactly as if the wolf was saying: See? That's how it's done. It's easy. Clayton growled, "Lie down and be still."

Since Wolf was sated with too much food and sweet rolls, he was sleepy and lay down obediently.

Clayton looked at Shelley.

The breakfast was cleared away and the first-aid station set up. "Any blisters?" She was primarily there for first aid.

The men showed every blister and even bits of rubbed skin, hoping they'd qualify for Shelley's sympathy. Clayton watched like a hawk. She was businesslike and quick. She didn't linger with any of them, and she didn't hold hands. She talked to the women. She was cool with the men.

Would she be cool with him?

The fires changed that day, and the untried crew was taken from their practice work and bused over quite a way to help.

The flames had climbed into the trees and the spectacle was awesome. They towered freely into the sky, beautiful colors, roaring sounds of crackling as the blaze went hungrily up the tall, straight trees with pistol shots of exploding resin.

For the new fire fighters, it was intimidating, at first. They were only between five feet to something over six feet tall, standing before a fire reaching up ten times that, twenty times that! But to begin to fight was to begin to win. Or to try.

It was hard work. Long hours passed with soot, sweat and dirt. The concentrated hours were endless and time was meaningless. Too soon they were pulled back. Retreating. A relief crew came. Houses were soaked by spraying trucks. And even as the crews wondered at the idiocy of building clear out there in the paths of all the varieties of nature's trials, they understood the lure of the beauty.

The pall of smoke was choking, and they used their masks. As they pulled back and rested, they saw grazing buffalo and elk in the meadows beyond. *Grazing!* In the face of that disaster?

But animals just moved aside for the fires. Very few were victims of it. They got out of the way and went on with their lives. They had no houses to be burned. They didn't sell logs. Their lines of communication weren't down. The fires weren't even inconveniencing the animals. It was only man who was disturbed.

At relief time, the crew didn't get back to their meadow. They were moved and near dawn, finally replaced, they dropped back and rolled into army blankets. When they roused, they ate tiredly in the pall of the smoke-laden sky, and went silently back to the line.

So it was almost a week before Clayton got back to their meadow. He'd said he needed to see about his violin and his wolf. Spears said he could go. "Yeah. I understand. You wouldn't want to lose either one."

But it was Shelley whom he sought.

The truck in which he'd cadged a ride, slowed enough and Clayton jumped off. He waved, and the guy tooted his horn in reply. Clayton considered the darkening meadow that looked deserted. Then he tilted his head up at the smoke-hazy sky that was less polluted, and the air breathed clean. It was like coming home.

There were a few spotlights, one over the empty table by the road, one by the deserted portable toilets down a way, and one by the first-aid truck.

She wasn't there. No one was there. Clayton whistled long and shrilly, waited, but no Wolf came. Where was his fiddle? *Where was Shelley?* He was completely alone.

It was so silent. Not a sound. He'd forgotten how noisy fire could be until it was absent. He figured he might as well shower and, being alone, began to remove his clothes on the way to the shower truck. Particularly tired now that he was so disappointed, he paused at the first-aid truck, then, naked, stepped inside the deserted station. He idly picked up things she might have touched. There were instruments, bandages and there were temporary casts.

They were lightweight and easily applied. He put one around his arm and snapped it into place. He snapped the second into place just as a car drove up. He turned his head, listening. Finally someone got out, and in the next minute Wolf was alertly at the truck door. He turned and yipped in an aside.

Clayton frowned. Wolf never made sounds. He was trying to bark like a dog? What was happening to his wolf? And *she* came into the truck!

He was so astonished that for a minute he forgot he was naked. He stared.

So did she. Then her face was agonized as she questioned softly, "Both arms?"

He was tongue-tied and turned his back, going scarlet all over.

She said, "Didn't they take you in?"

He was there.

She said, "Do you hurt badly?"

He was in agony. He dropped his chin on his chest in embarrassment. Then frantically he moved his chin along the catch to release the light cast.

"No! Don't do that. Let me see the chart. Hold still." She picked up a clipboard and scanned its paper.

He was paralyzed.

Reading from the paper, she exclaimed, "Poison *ivy*? Oh. That, too?" She grieved for him. "You'll need a full bath for..." Her voice trailed off. "If you wait for the hospital... It could be hours. You need to... be cleaned. You should be washed, now." Her uncertainty vanished and she was bravely firm. In control.

Something clicked in his mind. She would bathe him? He mumbled, "Yes," not moving so that he wouldn't frighten her.

"This will be hard for you," she said earnestly.

And he almost choked.

"But I am trained in first aid. I do know how to do this. I'll be careful of you. I'm sorry one of the men isn't here to help you, but they were needed on up the line. There was a whiplash of fire and a couple of the men were scorched. Poison ivy can't be any worse. It's too bad you can't shower. But that's impossible with the casts. Let me help you."

He held his breath.

"I'm sorry about your arms."

He nodded. She would touch him. She would put her hands on him. He would probably lose his soul for allowing her to believe he had two broken arms, but he could not forfeit this opportunity to have her close. To have her touch... His body reacted and he blushed painfully.

"It'll be all right. Don't be embarrassed. I'm like a nurse." She was firm and positive. Businesslike. She encouraged him: "It isn't brain surgery, you know."

She prepared the water and poured it into a pan. "Perhaps you should sit down. Here, sit on this towel. I'll just put this one on your lap." It bunched up unsteadily. "Yes. Uh. I'll do your head—your hair—first. Are you in great pain?"

His head bobbed in heartfelt agreement. But he was forced to be honest. "I'm sure my arms aren't broken." Ah, his tongue had hedged.

"You're very brave. There isn't any medication listed for you. Your name isn't even on this work sheet. Just that you must bathe fully. They don't mention your arms, at all."

"They're not broken."

She looked at the casts. "I do hope not."

"I'm okay."

"You're so brave."

He felt guilt weighing down on him.

"I have your fiddle," she said into the silence. She was busily scrubbing his hair.

It felt wonderful. He closed his eyes and just...felt.

"It's in my car, and I've wrapped it in a blanket to protect it."

"Thank you."

"My name's Shelley Adams. My parents named me for the poet. They are that sort. I live not far from here. I just bought the house. It has a pool! Maybe you... You might not see me here and not know where your fiddle is."

"Thank you," he repeated.

She lay his head back and poured warm water through his clean hair into a bucket on another chair. "I need to do your body. Can you stand all right?"

He stood, and she reached to catch the towel but it didn't fall. She rubbed her nose and turned her head away, then turned back and removed the towel. She glanced up, but his eyes were closed and he was again scarlet.

With liquid, she quickly soaped down his chest to his waist before she hesitated. She moved around him and began to soap his back. Her hands didn't linger or try to entice, but he was. He was appalled by his body's immodest reaction and stood rigid, wishing he'd admitted to his fraud.

She busily scrubbed his back, then reached around to his stomach. She did his buttocks, and through his legs to his sex. He almost went through the truck roof.

She gasped, "Did I hurt you?"

"No." His voice was strangled.

It was fortunate that she was in back of him, her arms around his waist, her earnest hands thorough. When he shivered and then shuddered, her hands stopped and she whispered again, "Did I hurt you? I understand...I've heard that men...that they are very sensitive."

He was unable to reply.

She went on scrubbing his legs and feet, then rinsed him carefully. In the silence, he peeked at her through his eyelashes. She was quite pink, but very earnest. She hadn't meant to stimulate him. She was just giving a person a bath to prevent a contamination of poison ivy. How was he going to get out of those damned arm casts? How had this ever happened?

His skin reminded him that her hands were still on him. She was soothing a lotion over him...all of him. He sat down.

"Are you faint?"

"No." His voice was husky.

She was staunch. "I need to . . . I must . . . You have to have this on you."

"Let's wait," he said very quietly, tenderly.

"I don't know how long it will be before someone comes."

He couldn't think of anything to say to that.

She was finished with him finally. He was also finished. Wrecked. She put a hospital gown on him and cleaned up the splashed water and—"I am careless. There's soap clear over here!"

He couldn't think of anything to say to that, either. He stood up.

"I believe you should sit down. How did you break your arms?"

"They aren't broken." Only then did he notice that Wolf was lying across the doorway of the truck, his chin on his paws, his eyes on the humans. He had a very tolerant look on his face.

She was saying, "I know that positive thinking can cure some ailments, but I don't think bones are in that category. You need to sit down. You're probably still in shock. I am curious how you got into poison ivy. There isn't much around here. Some along the Gardner River, and some over by Jackson—"

"It might not have been poison ivy."

"Well. It's best to be sure," she comforted him. "Do you itch at all?"

His tongue volunteered. "A little."

"Should I put some more lotion on you?"

After a long pause, he reluctantly shook his head very slowly. "Best not."

"I wouldn't mind."

But before he could say he would love it, the sound of a motor came to their attention, and a truck pulled up by the meadow. Wolf got up and vanished.

"Take care of my wolf, will you?" Clayton then could hunt her down if she was assigned to another place. He explained, "I may have to go in to the hospital to have my arms x-rayed."

"Wolf and I get along very well. How do you call him?"

"A sharp whistle." He demonstrated.

The wolf appeared briefly, but two men's voices responded. They came to the first-aid truck and raised their brows at the double casts. "What happened to you?"

"I'm okay." Clayton knew he couldn't fool anyone.

The men nodded and one said, "A steel man."

"Yeah."

The second man said, "Well, I guess we'll have to take you in for x-rays. That kind of cast doesn't help. They only get you to the hospital."

"They aren't broken," Clayton said quite honestly.

"Well," said the second man. "Somebody had reason to put them casts on you, so we need to see to this. Got a sandwich for us, honey?" With no reply, he said, "Hey. Shelley. Got a sandwich?"

"Oh," she exclaimed broadly. "I thought you were talking to the wolf."

"I don't call wolves honey."

"Some women do," she mentioned.

"Are you trying to put me in my place? You ought to know that's a hopeless job. Give it up. Would you please fetch us something to eat?"

"I'd be glad to."

She did that, and she fed Clayton. He wished the two men gone, so that he could wallow in her attention. Although she was still rather pink-faced, she was businesslike and helpful, and the men watched every move she made. They especially watched how he took the bites of food from her fingers. All that thrilling care, and he couldn't do anything about it. He swore a solemn oath that he would never again do anything sneaky in all the rest of his days. He would be honest and aboveboard.

She asked, "Does your head hurt?"

Clayton looked aside and down. "How'd you know that?" His head was bent a little and his body sagged.

"You frowned," she explain gently.

How clever of his forehead to have done that.

She lay her hand on his forehead. "Sometimes a broken bone will start a fever. You need to get to the hospital."

"We'll go now." The two men rose.

It was late. They'd already been to the hospital, and they were tired. Clayton was causing them a great deal of trouble and effort, all because he wanted Shelley to touch him. "I'm okay. Really."

"No trouble, buddy. We can't have our fiddle player's arms in jeopardy. We'll see to you."

Clayton reiterated, "My arms are okay."

"Good attitude," one said.

The other asked, "Can you walk all right?"

"I need my pants."

"No," Shelley said. "If you fell into poison ivy, your clothes must be washed in yellow soap. I have to bag and label them. You'll have to be issued new clothing."

One man smiled. "You get to wear the gown. Watch the drafts."

Clayton shook his head. "God Almighty, I can't let you guys make another trip into town."

"Our families are there." The other one opened his arms wide. "We'll spend the night with them. We'll check you out in the morning. If you're really okay, we'll bring you back. If you're stoved up for sure, we'll see what to do about you. Okay?"

Clayton's conscience was eased. He turned to Wolf, who was just outside the truck. "Come," he commanded.

The wolf eased in like a shadow.

Clayton put one cast over Shelley's shoulders as he watched the wolf. "Guard."

Wolf gave him a tolerant look for being redundant.

So Clayton rode into Jackson, watching how a truck's gears were handled. Being fire fighters, they were welcomed at the hospital, and everyone looked at Clayton's *two* casts with frowns. He said, "I want to see a doctor, alone."

That made them all curious. He wouldn't let them do anything until he'd seen the doctor. Clayton was adamant. An orderly tried to take his temperature, but Clayton was firm.

Finally a rather harried doctor came, and Clayton made him show some ID before he told everyone else they had to leave.

"Look," explained the doctor to Clayton. "This is the emergency ward. We can't get all these people out of here. No one is listening. What's the problem? Beside two broken arms," he amended. And sympathy was evident.

"Swear this doesn't go past us. I don't want nobody to know."

"What do you have?" The doctor's glance was sharp.

"Nothing."

The doctor raised his eyebrows. "What do you want of me?"

Clayton directed: "On the record just say, 'Bones not broken.' That's not a lie."

"Who put on the casts?"

"I did," Clayton admitted.

"Why?"

"I didn't expect anybody to be around," Clayton explained. "She came in, and there was an order for some guy to have a bath because he'd apparently found some poison ivy. I wanted her to touch me."

"I'm not surprised," the doctor said. Then he asked, "Was it Shelley?"

"Yeah. It could embarrass her."

"Shelley." The doctor's repetition was pensive.

Clayton nodded. "She thought my arms were broken. I wanted her to bathe me. And she did."

In some irritation the doctor asked, "How was it?"

"I'm not sure," Clayton said guilelessly to a fellow man. "I felt so bad to fool her, that way, that I was distracted."

And he finally caught the doctor's sympathy. "Okay. Let's get the casts off. I'll cover for you."

"Thank you."

"You be careful of her. She's a very nice woman."

Clayton was complacent. "My wolf is guarding her."

"Wolf?"

Clayton nodded. "That's his name, too. I raised him." It was as if the cork had been pulled from his tongue and the words flowed. Clayton became aware that he was talking to a stranger just like any other human being! He *could* do it. But would the ability last until he saw Shelley again? Could he actually talk to Shelley? He confided, "I've been a loner all my life. I didn't know how to talk to people."

"You're doing fine." The doctor was a little sour.

"With you it's been easy."

"I would have given five years of my life to get Shelley to bathe me." The doctor's tone was gritty.

Clayton frowned. "You, too?"

"Along with most of Wyoming."

"Is she married?"

"No."

"Good." Clayton appeared satisfied.

"She's a very independent woman. She's bought a place for herself up in the hills."

"She told me."

Sounding annoyed, the doctor asked, "She volunteered that to you?"

"She has the wolf and the fiddle."

"You're the fiddle player."

"Yeah. My grandfather taught me. It's my great-great grandfather's fiddle."

"So the, uh, Mastersons have been around these parts for a while?"

"Yeah."

"Well, take care of yourself," the doctor directed. "I hope you stay around, too. But I'll give you a run for your money with Shelley."

"Good gravy, you want her, too?"

"For some time."

Clayton frowned at the man. "I really mean to have her."

"So do I."

"Well, damn." Clayton frowned. "This is going to be harder than I thought."

"I hope it's impossible for you."

"I'm not wishing you any luck, either." Then he told the doctor, "I need to know your name."

"Michael Johnson."

"You won't go back on your word on this arm business, will you? I've put a weapon in your hands against me."

Michael stated flatly, "I fight fair."

"A man can't ask any more than that."

"You be careful of her," the doctor warned.

Clayton stood up. "I'd sure appreciate a pair of pants."

"I can see to that."

"Thank you for helping me not embarrass her."

"It's for her that I did it." Michael made that clear.

"I understand that."

The medic's voice was somewhat sour again. "Stay healthy."

"Thank you."

The doctor said, "I'd rather not see you again."

"I can understand that, too. Goodbye."

Dr. Michael Johnson shook his head once impatiently and disappeared.

A very perky little brunette came in and said, "I'm to give you a bath." And her eyes sparkled in teasing invitation.

"That's very nice of you, but I can give myself one. However, if you could find me a pair of pants, I'd be grateful."

She grinned very sassily and asked, "How grateful?"

And Clayton knew Dr. Johnson fought dirty.

Three

The brunette nurse brought Clayton some surgical greens of soft cotton. He pulled on the pants and shucked the hospital gown. He put the footies on and wiggled his toes in them.

The nurse stood back, watching down his body and asked, "Ever think of going to medical school?"

"No, ma'am." He pulled the top over his head, pushed his arms into the sleeves and stood there, his dark hair mussed, his green eyes enhanced by the green of the clothing.

She asked, "Where do you live?"

"In the mountains west of Yellowstone," he replied.

"In what town?"

"In a cabin."

She nodded thoughtfully and mused, "It might be worth it."

He blinked and looked at her blankly.

With a grin, she informed him, "My name's Maggie Franklin. You can get in touch with me here."

"My arms are okay."

She smiled. "So's the rest of you."

And he thought she might be flirting. Now was the time to practice. What was he supposed to say? He smiled back at her.

And she laughed a deliciously naughty sound that skittered over the surface and tickled in odd places. That shocked him. Shelley was the only one who was supposed to do that to him. Was he susceptible to women? He'd have to watch it. He gave a little half-bow and said formally, "Thank you, Miss Franklin."

"You're welcome, honey."

Shelley had said some women call wolves "honey." Was Clayton Masterson a wolf? No. He was a one-woman man. And Shelley Adams was that woman. He didn't smile at Maggie Franklin. He was cool and precise.

He found that fire fighters were covered by federal insurance and the government would get the bill. Hospital personnel asked that Clayton return the borrowed clothing, and he promised to do that. He left the emergency room and stood outside in the cool air waiting for any truck that was going in his direction.

Maggie came out and checked on him now and then. And he found himself replying to her really quite comfortably. She asked him questions about his early years in the mountains. It was easy to reply. He didn't have to instigate anything. Maggie did it. She offered, "Would you like to kiss me goodbye?"

"I'm spoken for."

"Oh?" Maggie raised her eyebrows. "Who's the lucky woman?"

"She doesn't know it yet."

"Then she's a fool, and a man living in a cabin alone needs a woman who isn't a fool but a nurse."

Clayton was gentle. "Some lucky man will realize that."

"If the blank-minded woman who has caught your eye turns out to be really stupid, come back."

"Thank you." He meant that. Her offer didn't exhilarate his life-support system as much as the fact that he could talk to her and not be tongue-tied. Maggie had given him the precious gift of confidence. He felt he would be able to talk to Shelley.

Eventually he caught a ride over to the correct highway and since he was in medical clothing he got attention. There was alarm: "What's up? Hey, Doc, why are you standing out here?"

And Clayton realized they thought something terrible was going on. He had to give the explanation, but he didn't mention the arm casts that were The Cause of It All. He insisted that no one go out of his way for him, and he finally caught the breakfast truck back to the now-empty meadow. Signals had been crossed, and they radioed in for new instructions while they ate their own breakfasts.

Sam, the guy on duty in the unpeopled meadow, joined the three in the truck, and as they finished eating he asked Clayton, "Operating today?"

"It was all they had that fit me. I got in poison ivy—" he had no choice but to give some explanation "—and my clothes had to be washed, particularly."

"I heard your arms were broken." Sam slid a slow grin to Clayton. "Shelley do that?"

Clayton warned, "Careful."

"Not broken?"

"Not broken."

Sam supplied Clayton with a new issue of clothing, and Clayton abandoned his brief stay in the medical profession. Then Sam inadvertently gave Clayton the greatest gift of all. He let him drive the pickup on the road around the meadow. "You don't drive?" Sam was amazed. "Man, how did you get to be your age and not drive?"

"I can't skateboard or ride a bike, either."

"No balance?" Sam questioned.

"No streets or sidewalks where I live."

And the man was stunned. "It's like meeting an aborigine!"

"I'm not Australian." So. Clayton was still a little literal.

After covering the basics of the pickup's gears, Sam allowed Clayton to practice. "Stay on the road. Don't go off onto the meadow. The surface out here is very delicate. Once something's been on the unprotected land, it takes years for the soil to heal. There are still the trails of wagon trains from over a hundred years ago. That's how long it's been. See? The Park Service don't allow bulldozers in Yellowstone. Not if they can help it. The land can recover from fire damage long before it can from the tracks from bulldozers."

"Got it." That reply had long been a common one on TV.

"There's nothing on the meadow road to run into. Try it," Sam encouraged. "Just don't go too fast, and pay attention. That's the trick of good driving."

Clayton tried it, and found the whole operation of driving just the greatest thing that had happened to him—besides meeting Shelley.

Then Sam drew a map of the area, and Clayton went out on the few empty back roads. Of course he didn't have a driver's license, so he stayed off the highways, and by the greatest of miracles, he saw the mailbox that said "S. Adams." Hers? And he stopped. Backed. And he sweat.

Could he talk to her? Could he be casual and slick like the men on TV? Could he start the truck if he turned it off? He eased the gears into place, turned the motor off and then started it again. It was magic.

He turned the key to off, got out of the truck, with more confidence, with some élan. He reached to settle his Stetson as all men did who habitually wear hats, and he wore none. His hat was with his gear, God only knew where.

He went up to her house and looked around. The sky was overcast with the fires' smoke. The weather was cool with the sun hidden. The house was in a partially cleared place. And the pool looked fake, sitting rigidly, sunk squarely into the ground so incongruously there in that natural place. The house was better. It was one-story, with a pitched roof to discourage collecting winter snows, and it had a nice porch. But it looked very obvious and open to a man whose family had lived privately, hidden in the mountains, for a couple hundred years.

Shelley came out of the house. "Clayton?"

He stared at her. She knew his name. She was real. It always seemed to him that she would vanish if he didn't watch her closely. She didn't appear to remember that she'd had her hands on him...intimately, that she'd given him a bath. Had it meant nothing to her? While her cheeks were pink and her eyes sparkled, she didn't blush or look away from him.

She was soft in a long mid-calf skirt and a long-sleeved blouse. The cloth was light-colored. She wore some sort of low-heeled shoe. Her blond hair was loose and blew around gently. He wanted to smooth it for her.

Then the *wolf* came out the door and sat down to laugh up at the man.

"Your arms are all right?" Shelley asked.

He nodded, his eyes filled with his goddess.

"Do you need me?"

She realized it? His lips parted.

"Have they come back to the meadow?" She waited, then gave up on his replying.

He shook his head. "I was driving by." He said that just like they did on TV. Like he'd been driving all his life. He felt a little sneaky pride.

"That's Sam's truck."

Clayton nodded.

"Come inside and have some lemonade?"

"Thank you." He reached to removed his hat and again found he had none. He entered her house and looked around. Then he smiled.

It was a home.

The wolf came and leaned against his leg, and he absently worked his fingers into the handy pelt. It was something to do in order to seem casual. He was grateful to appear normal. He searched for something to say, and blundered on the right thing, "Nice house."

Her face shone with her pride in it. "I love this place."

He looked around. She had obviously been working on it. Her furniture was old and treasured. Cared for. He had a rocker similar to that one, but his needed to be redone. Her sofa was neat and orderly. His had a sprung spring. He realized he'd been neglectful. Careless. He would be embarrassed if she saw his house before he fixed it up for her.

She invited: "Won't you sit down?"

But he followed her into her kitchen. He and Wolf. He noticed the wolf felt entirely at home. What was he doing inside? "What's Wolf doing inside?"

"Isn't he allowed in the house?" She was surprised. "He came in before I did."

Of course. He'd told the wolf to guard her. But staying inside was carrying it a little far. He ought to be out patrolling. Clayton bent down and whispered, "You turning into a lapdog?" But he said it so that Shelley could hear, and her chuckle filled little crevices in Clayton's soul.

She made the lemonade and offered him a glass with a sprig of mint. He took the mint and sniffed it. His mother had used that for unsettled stomachs or coughs.

Shelley suggested, "Put it in your glass. There's a little mint in the pitcher. I didn't know if you liked it or not."

"My momma used it as medicine."

Shelley nodded as if not surprised. "Your fiddle is safe."

"Good. Thank you. But I believe you're ruining my wolf." She only smiled, very amused. He asked, "Do you spoil . . . everyone?"

"It depends."

"On?" He'd seen a man encourage a woman that way on television. He waited, and he saw that she blushed. Why would she blush?

"It depends on the man." Then she looked up at him and riveted him.

Clayton thought that she loved the doctor? "I met him yesterday."

"Who?"

She wasn't talking about the doctor? He shrugged because he didn't want to reply who. If she wasn't referring to the doctor, why call her attention to him?

"Whom did you meet yesterday?"

"I met a slew of people at the hospital." And his tongue went on: "I had to wear the surgical 'greens,' they call them. When I was trying to hitch a ride back, people thought I was a doctor looking for help." He'd managed to say all that!

She nodded in understanding. "With all the fires throughout the whole western part of the country, no one knows what's going on. It's really staggering."

"Do you have a root cellar to put your things in?"

"No."

He frowned. How unprepared she was for disaster. She could lose everything. She must be a city girl. "You a city girl?"

"How do you know that?" She smiled a little.

"Anybody lives out around here is prepared for disaster. No cyclone cellar?"

She shook her head. "No cellar at all. The house is built on rock."

"A cellar should have been blasted out. That was done for the pool. What good is a pool? You're a sitting duck, like this. If the fires comes through here, you'd lose everything."

"I have the pool." She gestured. "I can spray the house and keep it wet."

"It might work." This was no time to scold her. There was nothing she could do this year. "Any caves around?"

"Down the south drop, there's one."

"I'd like to see it." Clayton took control. "Can we get to it?"

"Are you a spelunker?"

His eyes widened. "I know what you mean! Somebody that explores caves!" He explained in an aside, "I watch the Discovery Channel." Then he went on: "Nope, I'm not one. I was just curious if it was handy. Could we look?"

"Sure. If you're in a hurry, we could leave the lemonade here."

He looked at his almost empty glass. If he finished it now, he might not be able to get back inside and ask for a refill later. "Okay." He rose.

She caught up a jacket and put it on. He realized he should have helped her with the jacket.

The wolf followed as they left the house and went along a path to the edge of the drop. It wasn't a drastic one. In the winter snows, an expert could ski down the smooth part of it. But it was steep. In places there were gorges in which there were the expected trickles of water.

There was a natural path along the slanting surface. Once it had probably been well-trodden. That would mean it could have been a long-ago hiding place or a habitation. Clayton got a little excited.

He led the way, and she came along after him. That she followed thrilled him. He felt they were the only two people in the world. They and a wolf. A tamed wild animal was rather appropriate.

The cave wasn't easy to see. They followed the path carefully, and he remembered to help her across places that were difficult or where stones had rolled down. When they came to the cave, Clayton was surprised. It was just suddenly there. He wished for his gun.

There were no signs that anyone or anything had been there in several years. But you never knew if an opening was the only one. He told Shelley to stay back, and he looked inside. It went back a way. The wolf eased in, just as cautiously, his nose testing. Clayton was careful with each step, looking up and down, back and on either side. On the wall were faded traces blackened by fire. It had once been a habitation. When?

He had run out of light when Shelley called, "Clayton?"

He didn't remember to respond but just went back to her. And he startled her. She was coming inside, looking for him.

She gave a little yelp when he suddenly loomed before her and then she touched his chest and about paralyzed him. "I thought you fell down a hole."

"I was careful with each step. We need to come back with some powerful flashlight. This might be very interesting. And you could put things here and keep them safe from the fires. Is there anything you would regret if you lost it?"

She turned her head, examining the cave floor. She looked very vulnerable, very civilized in an exceedingly primitive place. His heart melted. Was there any of his heart left with him? How could she have it and yet he could feel it melt?

"I have a chair that's precious." She looked up at him.

"I'll bring it down here."

"Could you do that easily?" She appeared earnest.

"Yes. For you."

She needlessly explained, "The chair belonged to a very lovely woman in a nursing home whose name I drew to visit. She gave me the chair."

"I'll bring it here."

"When the fire season is over, will you come and carry it back to my house?"

"Of course," he promised.

She smiled up at him in that dim light. And he longed to kiss her. Should he try? He leaned forward very slightly, but she didn't move away. So he put his lips on hers very gently. She kissed him.

He was electrified. His breath changed. He felt like rolling a stone against the entrance and keeping her there.

Wolf came back from his explorations in a bored trot, interrupting them. He went to the entrance and sat down, being patient with them.

She wondered, "What did he see?"

He promised, "Another time, we'll find out."

"I have to get back to the meadow." She was reluctant to leave him. "The crew will be back tonight."

"Come show me which chair."

"You're going to do it now?"

"Yeah."

She gave him a smile that was a gift. He felt his muscles get stronger and his bones harden into steel. He felt he could do anything.

The chair weighed a ton and was awkward as all hell, but he wrestled it down into the cave. He mentioned to God that it would be nice if there was a landslide to cover the mouth of the cave so that he wouldn't have to lug the damned thing back up as he'd promised.

Shelley had followed. "I know this isn't at all necessary, but if something did happen, I would grieve for that chair. Miss Lavender was such a lady. So is the chair."

"The chair's a lady?" He questioned that. A battleship, more like.

"Yes." Shelley was very sweet.

Could he kiss her again? Could he kiss her again...and stop? He took a deep breath and rubbed his chest.

"Do you want Wolf to go with you, or can he come with me?"

Clayton loved it that she'd asked. "He can stay with you." He knew if he wanted the wolf back, he'd have to drag the stupid beast away from her by the scruff of his neck. Like his master, the wolf had given Shelley his heart. Did Shelley realize she had two males who loved her? She appeared to think she was still free. When would she know? When would she realize that she was trapped?

She followed him out to Sam's truck and the wolf trailed along showing no interest in going with his "master." Clayton's palms sweat a little as he got into the truck and inserted the key. Would it start? It did. *And he remembered to release the brake!* It moved nicely, bucking only once, and he roared off down the road just like in a car commercial.

So he hadn't kissed her a second time. He had seen Ron Reagan's special on cable that said a man needed to wear a condom. Clayton had never used one. He

needed to buy some...but not around there. He knew
even Gasp had condoms in the general store, but how
could he buy some where he was known? Everyone
would know he was interested in a woman and wonder about the woman. He'd have to get back to Jackson with money in his pocket. He hadn't had any in
the hospital gown he'd worn in Jackson last time. So
he needed to do something about protection for her
before he carried his courtship any further.

Did she realize he was courting her?

On television, the woman always seemed to know.
When the man kissed her, she wrapped her arms
around him and rubbed her body against his. Would
Shelley ever do that to him? And open her mouth on
his and kiss him deeply? That meant that their tongues
would touch. He really wanted to try that.

He missed the turn that he was supposed to take and
learned about reverse, since he had to back quite a way
before he could go correctly. He had to pay attention.
It was Sam's truck.

Clayton was careful and made no other mistakes.
There was the meadow, there was Sam, there was another truck.

Clayton pulled up behind it gently, showing off his
expertise. He turned off the motor, set the brake and
exited the truck like a veteran.

"Where in hell did you go?" Sam wanted to know.
"Is there any gas left?"

"Yeah. Half a tank."

"I'm glad to hear that."

"It was great." Clayton held out his hand. "Thank
you."

Sam shook hands. "I've ruined a natural man."

"You've dragged me into the twentieth century."

"Next, we'll get you to work on a computer and try for the twenty-first." Sam grinned.

Clayton laughed. He felt companionship with Sam. It was very nice. He loved a woman and had a friend. The Outside was great. Life in it was good. And yet again he wondered why his parents had chosen to live so isolated. He knew they'd both known how to drive vehicles. They'd once lived in the world. His mother had been an Easterner. He wondered, if they'd lived, would they have encouraged him to go Out?

The old crew arrived in the late afternoon. They were tired and dirty, but glad to see Clayton. There were called greetings to the Loner. "How are you?" "How's the arms?" And Clayton basked in the friendliness.

The crew went to the showers and changed clothes, putting the filthy, smelly discards into a truck, groaning with tired muscles. They plumped down to eat, not seeming to plan to move again that night.

Clayton had seen when Shelley and Wolf arrived, but while he kept her under his regard, he didn't appear to give her undue notice. He saw that instead of the soft shirt she'd worn that afternoon, she was dressed in trousers and a shirt, like those she'd had on before in the camp. As always with the others, she was businesslike but pleasant. She smiled across at Clayton, and he allowed that smile to soak into him. The wolf came by Clayton on his rounds after supper and allowed his former slave to stroke him.

There were requests for music. Shelley fetched Clayton's fiddle, giving it to him, and he asked the crowd, "What sort?"

"Peaceable." "Lively." "Soothing." There were almost as many called-out suggestions as there were people.

So Clayton gave them a concert. He began with the feisty songs and ended up with slow, peaceful ones. He did a great job of it, and there was contentment in the meadow.

He and Shelley were the only ones not worn out. And he would share the coming two days of rest with his returned crew. So Clayton helped with the cleanup. Then he took Shelley out into the woods and they walked under the hazy night sky, accompanied by the wolf.

She took his hand!

He couldn't breathe properly for a while. Then as his big hand warmed her small, cold one, he put it over into his other hand and put his arm around her. They couldn't walk that closely over the uneven ground, so he stopped. "You're the prettiest thing I've ever seen." His voice was so husky that it didn't sound like his.

She smiled. He could see that she did. But she tilted her face up to smile at *him* and that was all it took. He knew not to make it sloppy right away. He kissed her and it was glorious!

And her body against his was more than any dream could be. She was soft and sweet, and she didn't pull away. She didn't rub her body against his, but he pressed her close and that was just remarkable.

He lifted his mouth and looked at her very seriously. Her eyelids seemed heavy and her lips were soft . . . and waiting? She didn't move out of his arms to finish the embrace. So he kissed her again.

She didn't part her lips and touch her tongue to his. He wasn't sure how to attain that sort of kiss. He opened his mouth a little and his kiss got squishy. Then he touched his tongue to the crack in her lips and she parted them a little. His tongue coaxed, and she opened her mouth a bit more, and he got to touch her tongue.

That almost set him off like the skyrockets on TV during the Fourth of July. Now he knew what it felt like to have a fuse lit. His was lighted and he was afraid it would go off. He hugged her very tightly and groaned.

She put her hands up into his hair and played with it. That gave him all of her body, stretched along his, and he suffered with rampantly wild need. However he had no protection for her. Even if he could coax her to let him, he couldn't.

But he didn't stop the torment. He breathed hoarsely, his body straining with desire, but he didn't let go of her, and he took the kisses she would give him. He trembled and his heart raced, but he couldn't take his hands from her nor ease his body from hers. It was sweet torture.

He brought his hands up her body to the sides of her breasts, puffed by the pressure of his chest against hers, and he pressed the heels of his hands into those soft mounds.

She didn't appear to mind.

He ran his hands down her slender, curved back and allowed his stiffened fingers to press into the top of her buttocks. And she allowed that. She stayed against him, accepting his fevered kisses, allowing him quite a bit of freedom.

As he kissed her, he turned her body just a little away from him and took her breast into his hand to squeeze it nicely. She shook her head a tiny bit and moved her shoulders to indicate he wasn't to do that.

But she didn't break the kiss or move away. So he didn't. But he took the liberties that she allowed. And he was in agony with wanting her.

"It's bedtime." Sam's voice had come floating out of the dark.

Clayton's first reaction was fervent agreement. Then he jerked his head up and looked over at Sam. He was too far from them to see how intimately involved they really were. Sam had only seen that Clayton had kissed Shelley.

Shelley saved Clayton, whose tongue was still thinking about deep kissing. Shelley, said, "We'll be right there."

Sam left.

Clayton looked down at the placid wolf, who hadn't sounded the alarm, and chided, "You've eaten too many sweet rolls."

Shelley finger-combed her Clayton-tousled hair. "Why do you say that?"

"He's civilized and not alert and protective."

"He's been very good with me." She defended the laggard.

And Clayton could only think that in another way entirely, how good *he* could be with her.

They walked slowly back to the camp. Slowly, because Clayton couldn't move very well. There they parted with only a look. And Clayton went to his solitary bedroll. He lay with his hands behind his head and stared up at the hazy sky. He knew his life was coming along miraculously and soon it would be perfect.

It was a long time before Clayton finally went to sleep.

Four

On the first of the two rest days, the crew mostly slept. Some went home to check on family, but the majority were from a distance and they were contented to sleep and lounge. They really didn't visit and talk until late in the afternoon.

Since he had no reason to be that tired, Clayton made himself useful with the support crew. And he helped Shelley with first aid and laying out the food. That way he got to see not only Shelley but his ex-companion, Wolf. The wolf was tolerant and just a tad indulgent . . . to an old acquaintance.

Shelley shivered in the early hours.

Clayton frowned. "What's wrong?"

"It's cold this morning."

He smiled, his eyes concealed by his lashes. "Naw," he denied it. "It's just that you don't wear underwear."

"I do so!"

But in the drawer in Gasp, he'd seen the wisps that women wear. "Not real underwear."

She gave him a sassy look, but didn't reply.

"I'll show you what real underwear is, and then you can show me yours."

"Clayton!" she protested and shook her head at him.

"I'm only trying to help." He smiled. Talking to a woman was getting easy. He may have been too forward there, but she hadn't been really mad at him. He looked down her body. The cold had peaked her nipples. His hot body reacted to that and he wished for a private place to warm her private places.

She said in a very prissy way, "You must behave."

He widened his eyes and claimed in innocence, "I'm pure." And had made her laugh. That was heady.

"Where did you learn to play the fiddle so well?"

"My granddaddy. He was a fine old man, full of stories of long ago, and he had a keen ear for tunes. He taught me all I know about music. I don't know nothing about women. I mentioned that to granddaddy one day. I said, 'Tell me about girls.' That was before I knew not to call women 'girls.' I was ignorant. And granddaddy said, 'Out here the only way you're going to fiddle around is with a fiddle. There aren't no women out here a-tall, a-tall.' So since I don't fiddle with women, I only fiddle with a fiddle. I don't know nothing about any woman."

She scoffed and laughed. That helped him. And he smiled, so she disbelieved him.

As they worked together, he didn't touch her. He didn't put his hand on her shoulder or at her waist, and he didn't hold her hand. But he looked at her.

Working with her made that easy. He looked at the way she turned her head and how she licked her lip and the way she slanted her gaze to one side.

And he saw that she was perfect. A man just didn't need nor could he hope to find a more perfect woman. She was what he wanted, and he'd see to it that he was what she wanted. It was simple. He smiled at her.

"Why are you smiling?"

"I was thinking about kissing you."

"Clayton!" She pretended to be scandalized.

He knew she wasn't. Her cheeks pinked nicely, but it was because she was pleased he was teasing her.

"Your hair's so pretty."

"You're embarrassing me." But she put the back of her hand under the side of her hair and pushed it back a little.

He smiled because it was so easy to lure a woman. He'd have her soon, then she'd know about him, how it would be with him, and she'd love him. It wouldn't take any tricks, at all. He would just be himself, and she'd fall right into his trap.

He said, "Your body is beautiful."

But that rather shocked her. She didn't know how to reply.

"Was that too bold?" his clever tongue inquired by itself.

"Yes."

"But I think it."

She bit her lower lip, trying not to smile. So she wasn't really insulted.

"I'd like to carry you off into the woods. I'd like to take you to my place. But we'll have to wait a while to go there. It's right in the line, if the fires continue that way. I may lose it."

"That would be terrible." She was concerned. "Is the cabin the original one?"

"No, it's burned a time or two. It did when my folks had it. They went back there after Vietnam and rebuilt it. It's a good place."

She touched his arm. "I hope it doesn't burn."

"If it does, I'll rebuild."

She stopped to look at him. "Don't you even have a road?"

"No need."

"What if there was an emergency," she asked, "—and you had to get to a hospital?"

Clayton explained as if it was routine, "We cut a flat place for a helicopter. It's handy."

"What exactly do you do for your living?"

He moved a hand toward the landscape. "I live off the land."

"Uh . . . no pool?"

"Ours is a little cool." It was a wide place in a spring-fed stream. "But it's not far. And in the woods, that way, you can go skinny-dipping. I'd sure like to see that."

"There you go again," she scolded saucily.

"I'm an honest man."

"And a fresh one."

"Fresh out of the hills." He gave her a smug look, and she laughed. He had her right in the palm of his hand . . . almost. Soon now.

Spears saw to it that the crew had hot meals and the water truck came and refilled their shower tanker.

Spears told Clayton, "The water comes from rivers quite a ways from here. There are ponds close by, but they are so delicate ecologically that the forest service won't allow the removal of water from them for any reason, even to fight the fires.

"The water from our showers could alter this meadow. That's why we collect the water from the showers and reuse it with the fires."

Clayton shook his head once. "I didn't know keeping things natural from the tourist influx was so much trouble."

Spears agreed. "There are a lot of conflicting opinions about that. We should have let the land alone in the first place. Too many people want to see the pretty trees, because that's 'nature' to them. The real tragedy of these fires is that the rain forests are being deliberately burned off in the southern hemisphere at this same time. Think of what all this burning is doing to the atmosphere."

Clayton had watched a PBS program on that. "The greenhouse effect."

"Yes. If everyone in the world would just plant one tree, we might balance the loss of the rain forests."

Clayton looked around. "We talk about a 'long time ago' and it's been less than a couple hundred years and then it was only wagon trains leaving tracks. We've sure done a lot to louse up this world in a very short time."

"Yes." Spears had to agree. "At least we're becoming aware of it, and people are beginning to realize what's happening. *Time* magazine made the polluted world the 'Man of the Year' in 1989. We need more of the honest reports, ones that aren't bent to soothe."

"My parents had only me because the overpopulation was becoming apparent. Too many people. That's the sad part."

Spears added, "We have to do what we can to educate all the people of the world."

"How do you make the greedy and the selfish ones listen?"

"That's the crux of it all." Spears shook his head.

Sam came along. "Hey, Clayton, why don't we go into town and get your driver's license?"

Clayton laughed. "Sure. I'll drive."

"No. I will. I have to instruct you the whole way into town so you can pass the written test. You can write, can't you?"

"I got a man a wife with my writing."

"Did you now." Sam laughed.

"She's a jewel." He grinned at Sam as he thought about Stinky's husky, muscled, gap-toothed wife.

Sam was interested. "How about you writing a letter for me to send to my woman?"

"No. You learn to talk to her," advised the expert. "And you might find a mushy card or two to send to her for no reason." Clayton had that idea from a commercial.

"You can help me pick out a couple of cards in town, and I'll buy you a beer."

"If you let me drive back, that'll be enough. I can't drink beer."

"Deal." They shook hands.

Spears asked, "You let your license lapse?"

"No. I'd never driven. Sam's teaching me." He grinned and put a hand on Sam's shoulder. He looked over for Shelley and saw that, somehow, Dr. Michael Johnson was there. Clayton's sudden alertness to danger made his heart pick up its beat.

"Come on," Sam said easily. "Let's go."

Spears said, "Good luck on the tests."

Clayton replied, "Thanks." And as Spears walked away, Clayton growled to Sam, "What's that clown doing here?" Clayton's mother had called people clowns when they didn't agree with her.

"Who?"

"Michael Johnson."

"The doc?" Sam was surprised. "You know him?"

"I met him at the hospital."

"He comes around to check the resting crews," Sam protested. "He volunteers to do that. He's one of the good guys."

Sourly Clayton said, "Yeah."

"Wow. Will you look at that brunette? She's never been along before this."

"Her name's Maggie." Clayton supplied that off-handedly.

Sam drew back his head and gaped. "For a man who couldn't drive until yesterday, you sure do get around."

"What's Johnson doing talking to Shelley?"

With exaggerated patience, Sam reminded him, "She's the first aid."

"He isn't talking medicine."

Sam grinned. "Sounds like you're getting possessive. You know that I saw you with her last night. You were pitching pretty good there. She's never allowed that with any other man."

"No?"

"You've seen how she treats us," Sam complained. "We've all tried. How'd you manage?"

Clayton was silent, brooding over the good-looking doctor who was over there, putting it on for Clayton's woman.

"Come on, Clay. Let's go, and we'll be back for supper. Hustle up."

"I need to ask her to keep an eye on my fiddle."

"Hell man, nobody's going to be stupid enough to touch it."

But Clayton went over and got his fiddle from his pack and went back across the meadow to Shelley. He acted like an executive on TV who was in charge and no one would question his interruption. "Shelley," he said. "Would you mind keeping my fiddle? I have to go into town."

She smiled blindingly at Clayton, but he only barely registered it because he was so conscious of the man with her.

"Hello, uh, Masterson, isn't it? How're the arms?"

The bastard. "Fine," Clayton replied courteously to a nonentity. "I'll be back," he said to Shelley. And he walked away as if through glass double doors to attend a world-bending conference. He almost tripped over Wolf, who was sitting beside Shelley with his lip pulled up enough to show his fangs. Clayton smiled to himself. Wolf was protecting his property for him. Or was it just that Wolf was territorial? It didn't matter. Wolf had allowed Clayton to kiss Shelley, but he was showing his fangs at Johnson. Good wolf.

With a lighter heart, Clayton joined Sam. They went to Sam's truck and drove toward Jackson. All the way there, Clayton was drilled in the litany of safe driving. What distances should be between cars at what mileage reading, when to start signaling and when to begin to turn. Then Sam told Clayton when and how to slow down. Sam demonstrated. At a crossing Clayton was to look left, then right and *left again* before pulling into an intersection. All basic.

Clayton absorbed it. He missed two on his written, but he passed his driving test easily. He was exuberant. He was a driver! . . . and he would add to the pollution. That sobered him. It was a skill he needed. Nobody knew when he would need to know how to drive a vehicle.

The two went to a greeting-card place, and they went over all the friendship and lovers' cards. Some gagged Sam, but they did finally find two that he thought would be all right. He made Clayton pay for them. Acting aloof from such mushy stuff, Sam looked off out the doorway as the purchase was completed.

They then went to the post office and bought stamps, and Clayton waited with tolerant patience while Sam stood at the writing table in the lobby, agonizing over how to sign his name to the cards. Clayton wouldn't let him give up, so Sam did get them mailed.

Clayton was amused by Sam. He thought it was funny because Sam could be so macho and flippant about women who didn't matter, but he became paranoid and careful with one who did. Clayton knew that was dumb.

Clayton couldn't find any excuse to leave Sam and go alone to get some protection for Shelley. It made him restless to miss using the opportunity, but he could not allow any indication that he was that involved with a woman. Suspicion would fall on Shelley.

Clayton drove back to the meadow. As he drove, the feeling came to him that he wasn't an idle, useless convertible driver going too fast in a car commercial. *He* was a means of transport.

Sam drank the beer. But even Sam didn't pitch the cans from the car window. Clayton's attention was snared by that and he commented.

Sam shrugged. "You learn. They started recycling in my town. I went out to the gully in back of the house and pulled out sacks of cans for them. I got a case of beer with the proceeds." He enunciated the last word and laughed.

At the meadow, that damned Michael Johnson was *still* there, and he was going to stay for supper! There wasn't that much work for a doctor. After a couple of rubbed places, what was left? Shelley. Michael Johnson wanted Shelley...too. A woman can only love one man at a time. Clayton Masterson was the man for Shelley Adams. Just him.

Then the carrot-topped snickering lug of an Otis said to Clayton in a soft singsong, "Looks like your girl's interested in another man, Clay-ton."

That did it.

Clayton surged up from the ground and pushed the surprised Otis clear across about fifteen feet and slammed him against a tree. That did catch everyone's attention. Then Clayton picked Otis up above his head and whirled around, looking for a place to *throw* him. There were gasps and protests. Sam said, "No, Clayton!"

Then Shelley's voice said sharply, "Clayton! Put him down."

Still holding a subdued Otis aloft, Clayton slowly turned and looked mutinously at his love. She stared back indignantly. She was serious.

In the tense silence, showing off his muscle control, Clayton slowly lowered Otis down to standing, looking at Shelley the entire time. He was letting her know that it was only because she'd commanded him. Without another glance at her, Clayton straightened Otis's jacket and brushed off his shoulders. And he looked at her again.

She turned away like a Queen. And he bowed to her figure. But as he did that, Clayton asked softly, "Anybody else?"

No one made any kind of remark, at all.

He played the fiddle right after supper. He played the best he'd ever played, because the doctor was still there. He was playing to show off... like with Otis. Shelley needed to know he was a superior man. Not only that he was strong, but that he had sensitivities. On television, that was said to be important to a woman. He really ought to take her into the woods for a week to show that he could really take care of her under those circumstances, too. She might not agree to go. At least, not right now.

He'd surprised the crew so with his reaction to Otis that they didn't immediately react to the music. Then one of the women got up to dance with Sam. Sam had started it. He was Clayton's friend. And soon others danced. But of course the doctor asked Shelley to dance. Damn. Clayton should have known that would happen. His eyes never left them, and he hated that Shelley's body was so near to that other man's.

But what could he do? Nobody else played the fiddle. How could he put down the instrument and go dance with her? In the silence? Then Sam went to his truck and brought back a boom box. He came to Clayton to ask softly, "Want to cut in?"

And Clayton smiled at his friend. World War II movies showed men saying, "cut," and that way a man got to dance with another man's partner. Clayton would dance with Shelley. He wasn't sure how to do that exactly, but he would get to hold her.

When the piece Clayton was playing was over, Sam put a tape into the box and turned it on. It boomed out over the natural setting, and it was a wild and woolly rock piece. Everybody got up and wiggled and stomped and danced independently. The blocked-off road was a maelstrom of waving arms and gyrating bodies, and people laughed.

Clayton was appalled to see Shelley writhe so erotically to the music. What on earth did she think she was doing? He went over and said, "Cut."

Michael and Shelley looked at Clayton oddly since no one was really dancing with anyone else. The doctor laughed because Clayton's jealousy was so obvious. And the doctor's eyes glinted in challenge. Clayton figured Michael was a karate black-belt and expert. No man challenged another after such a demonstration as Clayton had put on with Otis—unless that man was pretty damned sure he could win.

Then Shelley took Clayton's arm, turned him toward her and "partnered" him. And the nurse, Maggie, took over the doctor.

Clayton realized immediately that Shelley hadn't moved in order to dance with him, but to "defuse" him. She was saving the doctor embarrassment. Or maybe she was saving his own face? She didn't smile at him or flirt. She just wiggled and jiggled and was as outrageously abandoned as all the other women there who were dancing so freely. Clayton thought the other women looked good. But Shelley was too mind-bogglingly sinuous to act that way. It wasn't decent.

He said, "Behave."

She looked at him in startled questioning. "I am behaving. It's you who has been acting wild, throwing people around, and barging into the dancing."

"It didn't mean anything, it's like tractor-pulling."

"Tractor-pulling?" She was incredulous.

"Tractors aren't bendable so with men it's more interesting," he explained all of his conduct very kindly.

"What are you talking about?"

"Tired muscles are stiff. Men then want to stretch and test them."

"That's why you were pushing Otis around?" She was incredulous.

"Partly." In a minute he told her, "You're jiggling." He looked off as if he only knew that through intuition.

"Good grief!"

"I knew you didn't realize—"

She blurted, "You are archaic!"

"I'm not!" he protested. "I'm not quite thirty."

"You act as if you've just come out of the hills!"

"I have." He was surprised she didn't know that. "I came down to help with the fires."

"I could *throttle* you!" Her dancing was more emotion than dance. She had clenched her fists and her eyes flew sparks.

He thought she was gorgeous. "Okay. Let's get out of this bunch and you can try. I would like you to. I need you to reassure me that you belong to me."

"What?" she gasped. "I do not!"

He waggled his head in impatience but he was tolerant. So she didn't yet really realize it. He'd loved her and obeyed her. What more did she need? He needed to buy some condoms. He told her, "I'll go into town tomorrow, and we'll get this thing settled once and for all."

"What 'thing?'" she wanted to know suspiciously.

"Us."

"What does that have to do with your going into town?"

He placated her. "I need to get something for you."

"A ... gift?" She frowned at him. "What?"

He smiled at her beatifically. "You'll see."

"You shouldn't spend your money on me."

"I'll share in it," he assured her.

"I don't want any presents."

"You'll want this." He watched her jiggle, then he smiled into her weighing, cautious eyes. She was worth the trouble.

With the ending of that piece, Maggie Franklin took hold of Clayton's arm and said, "My turn."

He heard Shelley's indignant breath intake like a balm on sunburn. He said, "Thanks, but I'm taken."

"Her?" Maggie asked in disbelief.

"Yeah."

Maggie judged Shelley. "She's insipid. She'll bore you stupid within a year. No humor."

"You don't know her the way I do," Clayton told Maggie with great kindness. "You'll find someone. Wait and see." He patted her shoulder like an uncle.

"I'll be around." Maggie turned from Clayton to give Shelley a dismissing look before she walked away.

Clayton happened to glance over and saw the doctor watching with amusement. Under other circumstances, Clayton thought, they might have been friends.

He took firm hold of Shelley's elbow and had to squeeze it because she did try to get away. He walked her away from the others and would have taken her back into the woods. It was dark enough, and he was brave enough to endure her alluring madness, but she did resist.

He told her practically, "Come along. I don't want to kiss you in front of all these people, but I will if you don't behave."

She snapped her words. "I don't see my conduct as misbehavior, but you are being completely out-of-hand!"

"Teach me to behave." He was so reasonable and kind, he thought, that she would soon melt. "Come along and kiss me, then you can begin."

"If you don't let go of my arm, I'm going to clobber you."

"I like a feisty woman." He smiled.

"You are beyond all sense."

"No," he assured her. "You're just reluctant to admit you're mine." He instructed her. "Women nowadays tend to think they like being independent. It isn't true. I've studied it on TV and while women want to *appear* that way, they're really tempting some man to step in and take charge of them. I'm willing to take you on. You'll tame down nice and easy. It's like riding a wild hor—"

"I am giving you one last warning!"

"Not ready?" He released her elbow. "Okay."

Shelley stood taking several breaths as she almost spoke several times, but she refrained and walked off.

Sam sauntered over and observed, "She got away."

Clayton frowned. "She's a bit balky."

Impatient, Sam admonished, "You can't treat courting a woman like training a horse, Clay."

Otis came up. "Clay, is she mad at you because of me?"

"No. She probably has PMS." Clayton sighed with the burden of understanding.

"A disease?" Otis looked aghast.

Clayton was exasperated. "Don't you ever watch television?"

"Is she going to die?"

"No," scoffed Clayton knowledgeably. "It's the monthlies."

Sam said, "You're only confusing him."

"Then you explain," Clayton suggested.

"I'll give him a book."

Clayton shook his head. "That won't help."

Otis protested, "I can, too, read!"

"Otis, let it go." Sam gave him a stern look.

Clayton began, "What I need is—"

But a big truck came to their meadow, and it stopped with a squeal. A man jumped down from the truck and ran, calling "Spears? Hey. Spears!"

"Ho! I'm here."

"You've got a smoke jumper. Masterson. Is he whole?"

"Reasonably."

"We need him. Where is he?"

And Clayton's ears heard Shelley say a soft, "No."

Men have to go to war and women have to sit and wait. That was the theme of all the old war movies. Such a fine truism had been spoiled by the women who wouldn't just sit. Look at those female fire fighters there in the meadow. They'd proven themselves. But he was a smoke jumper. He raised his arm in the silence. "Here," he said. It was satisfyingly dramatic. He felt like Walter Mitty having an adventure.

"Masterson?" the stranger questioned his identity.

"Yes." He stood straight.

"We're short a man. Could you fill in for us?"

And Clayton replied coolly, "No problem." TV's greatest quote.

"We'd appreciate it."

Striding firmly, Clayton went to the inquirer. He didn't salute.

"Ready?" the man asked.

"Yes."

"We need to brief you and get you in gear. We may have to go first light. You had the refresher?"

"Yes." Clayton was brief.

"Excellent. I believe the suspected spot isn't far from your place."

"The ranger?" Clayton's question was terse.

"We haven't evacuated him as yet."

"I know the area well."

"We're counting on that." The man turned to Spears. "Masterson may not be back to this unit."

"We'll see to his things." Then Spears elaborated, "His fiddle and the wolf."

"Thank you." Clayton turned to the stranger. "I'm ready."

"No fuss." He smiled. "A man after my own heart. Come along."

Clayton spared one glance to Shelley. She was biting a knuckle and her eyes were enormous. That was satisfying. He turned briskly away. It was a great exit.

He got into the truck, and they roared off. Clayton watched the gear-shifting of the larger vehicle. It was done differently than the gears in Sam's truck. Then a corner of his mind nagged, wondering if he'd ever see Shelley again.

Five

———

Clayton knew the two "jokes" shared among the smoke jumpers. The fact that they jumped out of planes that *weren't* burning into trees that *were*. And that they always carried an apple so that if they were caught in the invincible fire storm, they could put the apple in their mouth. Gallows humor.

Being somewhat literal, when Clayton had heard about the apple last year, he had first figured that the apple was for moisture, then that it would keep them from screaming. He'd never seen an apple in the mouth of a roast pig on TV. So maybe it wasn't that he was so literal but just that he lacked the basic experiences and folk-knowledge touchstones of the rest of the country.

And women. He was wry about his brief conviction that he could win Shelley with his instinctive reaction to her. He thought he knew women from TV?

They were another race entirely. And he felt a kinship
to Sam, who was so easy with all other women but was
scared over his words and conduct with the woman he
loved.

Shelley was going to take some study. But in the
meantime Clayton concentrated on how and when the
driver worked the big truck's gears, and that occu-
pied him until they arrived at the Loft run by the U.S.
forest service.

The group of jumpers was briefed, and since he
knew the territory so intimately, Clayton answered
questions. In the next day's first light, the reported
wisp was now a plume, slowed by the cold but turning into a column. The smoke jumpers got into their
gear, then into a DC-3 and took off.

Clayton really didn't like to take that step out of the
plane into nothing. He didn't mind flying or landing
on the ground, and he didn't hesitate to jump, but that
space between the plane and landing could be very
tricky.

From the first step into space until the jumper got
to the ground, anything could happen. With mountain terrain, the air currents were unpredictable; and
with the added turbulence caused by the fire's heat, the
winds were especially chancy. And because of *where*
they were needed, they always jumped into trees,
praying for any little clearing that might be around.

Every smoke jumper had his horror stories and they
traded them with relish. As bizarre as the stories were,
they were almost always true.

But this jump was to be into Clayton's own territory. This was his own place that was in danger. He
watched in the DC-3's pass-overs and picked the place.

Clayton jumped first of the five. That wasn't bravado. He just knew where they ought to be.

The decent was uneventfully scary. They landed, collected their dropped gear and got organized, then they wasted no time getting busy. They worked furiously on the line with their unique spade/pick/shovels, trying to keep the fire horizontal. It almost got away from them. They didn't win that one until long after midnight, almost sixteen hours after they'd jumped.

They were dirty, worn out, and they stank. They pulled back and watched, taking turns patrolling the line. Then at daybreak they went to the pickup area to wait for a chopper.

"You live out here?" one asked.

"Over that way."

"It's really beautiful."

Clayton turned away to see it, but he forgot to reply. He was seeing what he'd always seen—the seemingly untouched beauty of that world. Clayton looked back at the man who'd spoken, but he was talking to someone else.

The chopper came, and the jumpers were flown back to the Loft, to eat, strip, shower and sleep. After ten days and three more jumps, the Loft was again at full strength, and when Clayton came in tired and stinky, he was thanked for filling in, "May we tap you if we get short again?"

"Yes." He was being discarded.

"Tomorrow you can go back to your group." The man smiled. "Then we'll know where to find you. There's a truck heading that way in the morning."

Clayton said, "I'll just go along now."

"You ought to sleep here. You guys are dead on your feet."

"No problem." That good TV reply.

So Clayton shed the Loft gear and pulled on his own. He didn't bother to shower, he just wanted to get back to Shelley.

It took him that night and a hunk of the next day, sleeping in the trucks that gave him rides. He walked some of it, wondering if the meadow would be vacant again. But they were all there on the tag end of a two-day rest.

He was welcomed that evening, and given every opportunity to tell about the smoke jumpers, but he didn't realize he needed to weave experiences with the others and just replied, "It was hard work. Just like you guys do. We just get there a different way."

It wasn't enough. The others already had other experiences in common and spoke of those. Clayton didn't question so that he could share in them, for he'd never learned how to do that. And again, he was an outsider. He didn't fit. He felt that he was no longer a part of the group.

Worn out, he sat on his reissued bedroll in another meadow, to watch as Shelley worked during that session of first aid.

There were very few work blisters now. Their hands were used to the constant effort, and their bodies were adjusting to the different movements required of them. The members of the crew moved easier and were stronger.

They ate prodigiously. They talked and questioned and shared. Wolf came over to Clayton and laughed at him. Clayton hugged the animal tenderly, remembering how he'd found the cub and struggled to help it survive.

The wolf was tolerant but went back to Shelley.

Finally She came to him. "Hello, Clayton." It seemed that she really didn't want to talk to him. She looked around at the others and was uncomfortable.

"Hi."

"Are you all right?"

"Yes." He thought that she was being a little cool toward him. Had she been with the doctor while he was gone? She didn't look right at Clayton but beyond him or across the meadow. Who did she search to see? "You'd best be upwind of me." He drew her attention to himself. "I'm a little ripe." Clayton wanted to remind her that he was a warrior home from the wars. He had given up a night's sleep to get back to her, but he didn't tell her that.

He thought that she didn't appear to *want* to notice him. She studied her fingers and looked up into the sky, and she moved around as if she was impatient. But she didn't look at him.

She asked, "And you're back with us, now?"

"Yes." But when he said that, she didn't appear glad. She looked off to one side of him and licked her lips restlessly. She didn't even seem to realize that he was watching her. What had happened to make her twitch that way?

"Well ... How are your arms?"

"Fine." They could crush her soft body to him while he kissed her and sent himself into madness. What would she do if he did that? Would she screech and struggle? And he remembered how it had been that night in the woods when she'd allowed not only kisses but touches. And he could think of nothing more to say.

She hesitated. He looked about to see if Michael Johnson lurked anywhere around. Maybe she wanted to get back to him.

"Well..." She seemed at a loss. "I have your fiddle, you remember."

"Yes."

"I suppose you're too tired to play tonight."

She thought he was a wimp? That he couldn't handle anything, at all? But he was dead on his feet and couldn't pretend that he was ready for any real activity. He needed to strike a balance before he fell flat on his face. "I'll play one piece."

She smiled a little and said, "I'll go get it." And she was gone from him. Just like that. She left to fetch the fiddle as an excuse to quit talking to him.

His burdened soul groaned with despair. How could he have left like a hero and returned like some stray that wasn't wanted? He looked around for Sam. There was no sign of him.

Subdued, Clayton lay back on his bedroll feeling more alone in that peopled meadow than in all of his years on the mountains. At least then there had been a dream of finding a woman who could love him. Now he felt that dream was lost. Without Shelley, there could be no other women for him.

She came across the meadow with the fiddle and several others followed along with her, walking more slowly, interested.

As the light faded away into darkness, Clayton took the fiddle from her. She smiled right at him and wrinkled her nose. "You *are* ripe!"

He was offensive. He should have stopped and showered. He'd been so bent on getting to her. His lashes covered his troubled eyes.

"Were any of the jumpers hurt?" she asked in a concerned manner.

Why had she asked that? He shook his head. Only he was hurt...by her. He listened to the murmur of the strings, then he played his best piece. It was nameless by any but the name his grandfather had called it: "Unrequited Love."

Clayton had been grown before he'd known what the word actually meant, and he'd felt empathy for the one who'd written such soul-tearing music. He knew the composer had suffered. Once when he'd played that song, his mother's eyes had filled. Clayton had said, "He'd felt the pain."

His mother had looked at Clayton with the tears on her lashes. Then she had asked, "How do you know it was a man?"

Rather distantly thrilled by the strong emotion that must have created the music, Clayton had been positive. "It would take a man to suffer like that because of a woman," he had replied in his youthful ignorance.

"Ah," his mother had commented softly, "to be so young again."

Clayton only now understood his mother's words. But it wasn't a woman who'd brought the song into that meadow, it was a grieving man. Him.

Clayton made the fiddle weep. The strains of music touched the hearts of all those who could hear. It was as if Clayton played to the fire-touched wilderness. It was a song of great regret.

He looked at Shelley, so that she would understand his grief for her, and he could see the tears on her lashes just like those that had filled his mother's eyes. So Shelley, too, could feel emotion. Why not for Clayton Masterson?

He drew out the last sad note and there was silence.

Clayton put down the fiddle and rose to his feet to go shower. His own eyes were filmed with emotion, and he moved. But Shelley sighed. "Oh, Clayton, that was so sad."

"Yes."

Then someone called, "Don't leave us like that. Play us something to give us hope."

And Clayton was surprised. "It was grief, not despair."

Someone else asked, "Is there a difference?"

"Yes," Clayton replied.

But there were those who said, "No."

And Shelley put her hand on Clayton's arm and immobilized him. She came closer and said, "Give us a happier song, or we'll all cry."

Why shouldn't they? But even as he thought that, he knew he didn't want her tears. He gave in to her. His grief would be his own. "All right."

He played a courting song. One where the higher notes taunted and the lower ones threatened and then both sounds melded into quick, sassy teasing. You could almost hear the words on the singing strings, and the sounds made the listeners all laugh.

And wiping the grief from her eyes, Shelley laughed with them. Clayton was glum. He wanted her pensive. Why should she laugh, when his heart was ruined?

With their applause, he bowed, but he put the fiddle away into its wrappings. Then he straightened tiredly and clomped over to the shower truck, carrying a change of clothing.

As he passed his audience, they spoke and touched him. His sad heart wanted to lift, but he kept a heavy gloominess down hard on it.

He stood in the hot shower much longer than he should have. And when he turned it off and pulled back the curtain that contained the spray, there stood *Shelley* with a towel. She handed it to him opened out so that it concealed his naked body from her eyes. And then she leaned up on tiptoe and kissed his mouth quickly. She said, "Welcome back." And she turned and went away!

He was stunned. He was astonished. He was amazed. He dried himself absently. Then he dressed in a dream. She had been that bold. She'd come into the showers *knowing* that he was in there and naked. She had done that to be out of sight of the others, and *she had kissed him voluntarily!*

What should he do now?

He left the truck slowly, trying to figure how he should act, but she wasn't there, outside. Then he looked over and saw that her Jeep was gone. She had kissed and run away. Like Georgie-Porgie.

Very puzzled, Clayton went slowly, tiredly across the meadow and crawled into his bedroll. He lay there puzzling her out, but she completely baffled him. She had appeared not at all interested in him when she'd first come over to him, then she'd come into the shower truck specifically to kiss him. That seemed a complete turnaround to Clayton. Women were a great mystery.

He slept.

And dreamed.

All of his dreams were of Shelley and all were remarkably erotic. He burned through the night, never finding relief. So he slept poorly and wakened groggy. Women were a pain.

In the morning she was there, looking bright-eyed and rested. She was doling out the food as if she had no problems. She smiled and was cheerful. He could have wrung her neck. He clomped over toward her and the courting song came strongly into his mind. There she was, laughing that trill, while he was feeling all cross, deep notes. And he smiled.

She looked up and caught his gaze, and she blushed.

Why did she blush? Because last night she'd come into the shower truck and could have seen him naked again? Or was it that she too had had the dreams he'd had? He'd seen a PBS program on telepathy. Could his intense thoughts have made her share those hot, hot dreams? He hoped so. She ought to feel as frustrated as he. His body felt as if it had been scalded. He hurt for her. He had to get into town and buy some condoms.

Spears said, "Well, Clayton. It's good to see you back again. They called from the Loft. Said they'd worked your tail off and you would need some time. Take a couple of days. We can't work the volunteers into the ground. It looks like this September weather is going to keep on like it has, and without any rain, it could get really bad. Pray for an early snow. Without something like that, we could need you later more than we can use you now. Why not go into town for a couple of days?"

"Thanks."

"Shelley, I need some supplies. Are you supposed to be anywhere else? It looks like the crew won't be back for a week. I need to check on a section north of the park. Could you ask for these things to be delivered here in five days? And we need the tank truck filled. Would you see to that?"

"Certainly, I'll call in the orders early tomorrow," she replied to Spears. Then she turned to inquire of Clayton, "Would you like a ride into town?" She busily didn't look at him. "I'll be going in."

"I . . . yes. But I need to go up to my place and be sure it's all right."

Spears said, "Heard from the ranger just over a way from your place. He says it's looking okay so far."

"Thanks." Clayton was uncomfortable. He would go into town, but only briefly. How could he manage that? She'd only offered him a ride into town. If he drove in with Shelley, how could he get back to the meadow? With the shift of the fire threats, the meadow was off the truck routes.

Spears said, "Oh, and Clayton, here's your check for the first two weeks. They're always a little behind paying. Sorry."

He had cash. He'd had enough on him, but he looked at the check and was pleasantly surprised. He knew the week as a smoke jumper would be better. He could buy what he needed and have a nice little nest egg for the "sillies," as his dad used to call his mother's purchases.

He wondered what sillies pleased Shelley. If he went into town with her, would she let him drive? If he did, could he stop her car, take her into his arms, hold her close against his hungry body . . . and kiss her? He'd better not do that on the way into town. Not until he had the condoms. It would be safer not to kiss her until then.

He breathed carefully and rubbed his chest to calm himself, not hearing the directions and lists that Spears was giving Shelley. She appeared not the least bit perturbed that she would be riding in the same car with Clayton Masterson, the needy man who loved her above all else in this world. And it was a full love, not just a friendly one. He wanted her very, very badly. Really bad. Killing bad.

Why couldn't she give him a sly look, or act a little nervous or excited? After all, she was the woman who had boldly come into the shower truck and handed him a towel. Think of the risk she'd taken! If he hadn't been quite so wrung out then, he might have seized the opportunity and backed her against the wall, and shown her the difference between them.

He'd watched a guy on a TV late show offer that knowledge to his woman. He'd told the woman that she was treating him the same way she treated her women friends, and he was no woman. She'd said he was so sweet to her that she hadn't realized he was different from her *other* friends. So he had offered to show her the difference. That had made the woman pay attention. And the man had backed the woman up to the wall. On the screen, Clayton had only gotten to see their faces as they had kissed and panted, but he had suspected what they'd been doing.

Clayton tried to see himself doing that to Shelley. Naw. He wouldn't have. He still didn't have the condoms. He did need to go into town.

"Are you ready?"

Shelley was right by his shoulder and she was looking up at him with a little smile that appeared expectant. Clayton was rattled. Ready? Hell, yes! How had she known? His lips parted—

"I know you can drive, would you like to drive the Jeep?"

She made him feel unstable. He swallowed and said a husky, "Yes."

Spears had left. Apparently he'd gone while Clayton was immersed in his erotic imaginings. How embarrassing. He felt like a gorilla. No finesse. Clumsy. Uncivilized. He vowed that he would treat Shelley as a lady should be treated . . . clear into town.

However, as he drove away from the meadow, she said, "Could we stop by my place for a few minutes? I need to change."

He almost knocked his knee into the dashboard. He said, "Awwk."

"Fine. Do you remember how to get there?"

"I'm not sure." Hell, he was instantly sure that he couldn't remember his own name! It was . . . his father had called him . . . knucklehead. Right.

He followed her directions automatically, and they did arrive at her house. He could remember then, how he had gotten there, because she had been so precise about landmarks to watch for along the way. She had been very clear about them. Did she assume that would mean he would be coming back? "I'll wait here."

She paused. Then she turned back and looked at him. "Come on in. We have to leave Wolf here when we go into town."

"Yes."

Clayton slowly followed and felt stiff as a board. Was he alarmed? The innocent sacrifice? He decided he wasn't scared. He could handle it. She meant to seduce him. Why else would she want him to come inside? Yes. He rubbed his chest again and breathed. She was going to make love to him, and he wasn't prepared. Well, he was willing to go as far as she was. What would she do? How would she...

She commented in a friendly manner, "It's clearer up here."

He was a little behind her, and she'd looked back over her shoulder to smile at him. He said a nothing "Yes." She opened the door and led him inside. Clayton into The Lioness's Den.

She asked, "Did you miss me at all when you were gone? You never called or anything. Did you meet some of the women, and did they dazzle you?"

She was jealous? "They were okay. I did. Miss you," he added awkwardly, waiting breathlessly. When would she make her move?

"I'll only be a minute."

Then she vanished. He felt really disappointed. He'd thought she...he'd thought...

Her muffled voice came through the bedroom door. "Darn. Clayton? I'm caught. Can you come help me?"

Ah-hah!

"Are you decent?" He smiled, put his hat on the table and went to his destruction with great interest, quick breaths and an excited body. He pushed open her bedroom door and looked at her.

She was bent over, her bare back was a lovely curve, her breasts hung jiggling, her shirt was pulled over her head. "Well, now..." He wasn't clever tongued. What did a man say that would titillate a woman in these circumstances? Encourage her? Could he say that she needed no ploys, that he was willing?

"It's about pulled out by the roots." Her muffled voice sounded distressed.

Then he noted that her hands were caught inside the wrong-side-out shirt and she was trying to free her hair. "Here." He soothed. "Hold still. Let me." With great reluctance, he pulled her shirt back onto her body and her red face appeared, but her eyes were teary. "Aww. It'll be okay in just a minute," he assured her.

"The stupid button."

"I'll smash it," he promised.

She gulped a little giggle that charmed him to his toes. He worked to free her hair, first being sure it wasn't pulling. He hushed her suggestions to cut off the button, then to cut off that part of her hair. "No." And he worked it gently free.

"Thank you. I'm glad you were here."

"Me, too." He rubbed her scalp gently. "Is it okay now?"

"Just about."

He kissed her head.

But she moved, sliding her arms up around his shoulders and to the back of his head. And she offered soft lips to his.

His mouth was hard and hungry and he kissed her socks off. His, too. He held her as he hadn't since that time in the woods. And his body was starving for the feel of her. He held her so tightly that she had to pant, and she moaned.

He said, "I'm sorry, honey, but I just missed you so bad."

"Don't let go!"

"Ufff." His breath went out of him as if she'd hit his stomach. She *wanted* to be squashed up against him! And he had pulled her shirt back *down* over her luscious body.

His arms went around her and his hard hands roamed around, scrubbing at her body. His mouth was on hers like he was getting the last of a cherry soda through a straw. But then her little tongue peeked out and poked at his mouth, so that he opened his in erotic shock. She made a very sensual sound and his tongue went to play with hers.

Their kiss became inflaming. He shifted and twitched and moaned, and she made greedy noises. He shivered, and she wiggled and strained against him, and she didn't protest when his hands became really bold and adventuresome.

So he carefully lifted the bottom of her shirt. When she made no objection, he pulled it off and looked at her in awe. She was real. But she didn't stand there and allow him to look his fill. She began to get him out of his shirt.

He lifted his head back and gasped air and panted. Unsteady and trembling, he said, "It's been you starting all those fires. Who've you been kissing?"

She said very prissily, "Just you."

"You set me on fire," he warned. "And I've got nothing to protect you. You ought to back off until after we go to town."

"I went to town yesterday."

He blinked. "You don't have to go to town? You just said that?"

"I wanted you to come here."

He pulled his serious, still face back from her and asked carefully, "Why did you want me here?"

"So that you'd . . . kiss me."

"I can sure as hell do that." And he did that some more.

When they came up for air the next time they were more disheveled, more breathless and a little disoriented. But Clayton was clinging to a question which he did manage to ask, "And then?"

Heavy-lidded eyes looking up at him, she murmured, "Then I wanted you to make love to me."

Six
___

Clayton stood riveted. He stared at Shelley in something like shock. "You want...to make love with me?"

That startled her. "You...don't?"

"Oh, yes." He barely breathed the words.

"You do?"

"Yeeesss." He was so positive that he had trouble letting the word go.

Slowly she relaxed, and more slowly a little smile began to form. Then her eyelids drooped as she said smugly, "I did think you might."

"What made you think that?" he asked in awe.

"When we were in the woods, you did seem to be interested."

He frowned. "Only then? Not since? Now?"

"This did help. When you didn't call me or anything in that long, long time you were with the jumpers, I thought you were a hit-and-runner."

"Hit-and-runner?" That was used for wrecks. "You thought I'd wreck you? I was a wrecker?" His use of the word had made her meaning understandable. She'd have been wrecked without him? Then he smiled.

"There are men like that," she declared.

Being a TV expert, he assured her, "And some women."

"I suppose that is true."

"But not you?"

She blushed rather painfully and looked down. Then she said a tiny, "No."

He felt as if he were invincible. He needed to reassure her. "I'm not a wrecker, either. I'm careful."

"Careful?"

"I know about condoms."

She blinked.

"But I haven't been able to get into town and get any for us. If you will lend me your car, I'll go now. And I'll fill it with gas." He added that, because Sam had told him that if he ever borrowed a car, he should refill the tank.

She again began to smile faintly, but she blushed still. "You don't have to."

"Sam said I did."

She was back to blinking. "Sam said . . . what?"

"To refill the gas tank."

She nodded twice, but she added, "I went into town while you were with the jumpers. I bought the condom then."

He was stunned. She was a bold woman. "Why, Shelley—"

"Well, I wasn't sure you had any and I wanted . . . I knew we'd . . . I *thought* we might . . ."

She was unsure. He smiled down from his superior height onto his fragile and unsure woman. "I'm glad you did. Where are they?"

" 'They?' "

"What did you get?"

"One."

"Oh."

She was back to blinking again. "You would want . . . more than one?"

"Maybe." How was he supposed to know? "Let me see it."

"I put it in the closet."

He realized then that she had meant one *box*, one that was big enough that it had to go into the closet. He felt a little faint wondering how voracious she might be.

Still without a shirt, she took a chair and pulled it over to the closet door. Her sweet breasts shimmered with her movements, and he was distractedly enchanted. She opened the closet door and adjusted the chair. Clayton walked over tautly interested. What on earth?

She got up on the chair and reached for a hatbox, her body stretched nicely and her breasts jiggled a little making his breath pick up noticeably. She opened the box, lifted out the hat and took out the foil-wrapped square. She handed it to Clayton shyly.

One condom. "In the hatbox?"

"Sometimes my mother comes as a surprise." She shrugged, looking tempting in her seminude state. She made him feel very tender. She wasn't a wild and woolly woman. She was afraid of shocking her mother.

He started away, but she didn't get down from the chair. He turned back and looked at her standing there in just slacks. She was a picture for any man's eyes. Was she waiting for him to help her? Her knees were close together and her face was pale. "Are you afraid of heights?" It was the only thing he could figure. "Here, let me help you down."

He gave her his hand and watched her feet step gently to the floor. Her hand was cold. He glanced up at her face and she continued pale. "What's the matter?"

She gestured vaguely. "With all the talk and—" she gestured again "—everything, I...well, I haven't lost interest, but I don't think now is the time to do this, after all."

He confessed, "I don't think I could get it on anyway. I've...I don't think I could."

"You don't want to?"

"Oh, yes," he assured her very sincerely. "But like you said, maybe not right this minute." He checked out the packet and there were no directions on the back. He licked his lips. He just thanked Ron Reagan, Jr. for that TV hour on AIDS, because on that show the kind and practical Ruben Blades had used a banana to show people like Clayton Masterson how to put on a condom. Now Clayton did have a condom, but he had none of the recommended spermicide.

Life got complicated. It was easier, alone on the mountain. Clayton looked at Shelley. She was standing quietly, her forearms modestly over her breasts as her hands unnecessarily busied themselves with each

other. She was shy, really, and well worth any hassle.
Just to look at her was worth the struggle. To actually
make love to her . . . well, that would be a miracle.

He took her cold little hand and kissed it. He'd seen
it done any number of times on TV, and he did a fine
copy of the best. She allowed it, but she was a little
hesitant. She probably thought he was going to . . .
jump her. On TV, that was the word the swingers, the
hipsters, uh, the in crowd had used for a a while. Jump
her bones. What a dumb way of putting something so
amazing.

He thought he might get the condom on then, but
when he considered Shelley, he realized that she was
still enduring the attack of shyness. That was soothing to Clayton. He wasn't the only one who was hesitant. He had no idea how to go on past kissing and
hugging Shelley. He'd never had a woman.

He'd never gone to school. His mother had thought
it was vital for him to go to public school, but there
was simply no getting there from their cabin. And he
didn't want to leave the mountains. The one time
they'd tried boarding him in town, he'd been home the
next day, his feet blistered raw by the new shoes. His
mother had cried with soft sympathy, and his dad had
held his shoulder for a long time. Clayton had learned
from a correspondence school, monitored by his
mother and dad. He'd managed.

But he had known from watching TV that he'd
missed a lot of experiences in not going out into the
world. Still, when he had found the tenderfoot, lost in
the mountains and starving right in the middle of all
those things he could have eaten, Clayton had wondered which was better? After that, he wasn't at all

sure that civilization was the answer...at least not for him.

"I'm glad you like living out, away from town," he told his love.

"It's noisy out here," she complained. "I came out for peace and quiet, but it's just different noises than those in town. Some are scary."

"What noises?"

She made a vague gesture. "The wind. The trees. Coyotes. All sorts of creatures. And people! Along the south lip of the drop-off, occasionally there are even hang gliders! They come on you—surprise. Suddenly there's this huge shadow, bigger than a California condor and without a sound, some nut sails overhead on the air rising along the drop-off. No place is safe anymore."

He nodded. "We get the ultralight planes now and then. The animals can't believe them. Once I had to find a guy who had crashed. He was a mess, I had to carry him out on my back, to one of the meadows."

"What happened to him?"

"He recovered okay. In fact, he came by to see me. Landed one of those mosquitoes on our helicopter clearing and dropped by just like it was next door. I can understand the old-timers who didn't want somebody living just twelve miles away and moved on farther west. A man from Indiana did that."

She hesitated. "Are you...antisocial?"

"Against people?" He watched as she put her hands in back of her, and he could look at her. He felt very social. He sure as hell wasn't a loner. "No. I just don't know how to be friends. I've never had the practice."

"You do very well," she assured him.

"I don't feel a part of . . . humanity. I feel like I'm a . . . an oddball."

Very earnestly she told him, "You're one of the most talented and kindest men I've ever known. And you're very brave. When we thought your arms were broken, you were so staunchly positive. That takes real fortitude. I'm proud of you."

"Well . . ." This time he was the one who blushed. God. Sometime he was going to have to tell her why that had happened, and he dreaded her reaction to his farce. "It was worth it," his tongue put in. "You gave me a bath." Clayton was appalled. What would she do now, throw him out?

"Was that awful for you? I really liked doing it."

Just recently showered, Clayton sniffed at his arm and said, "I could use another." His grin was lascivious.

She put her hand to her mouth and laughed behind it, her eyes dancing. "Would you, really? Would you let me?"

She thought it a privilege for her to bathe him? "Only if you'll let me bathe you."

"Oh . . . no-o-o! I couldn't do that!" And she laughed with wicked humor.

"If I let you do me, then it's only fair that I get to do you." He reached for her.

She backed away sassily. "But that's different."

"It sure is. Let's get me out of the way, so I can do you."

"That's scandalous!" she protested.

"Think of it as helping in my understanding the human race." *He* had said that! How had he thought to say that? Brilliant! And he grinned as she went into a bunch of out-of-hand giggles, jiggling delightfully.

He just stood there, looking at her sweet feminine body and listening to her lovely feminine sounds. Wonderful. She was a wonder. "Want to finish undressing me?"

Apparently women found that fascinating... according to television. Women liked undoing shirt buttons. And Shelley came to him rather shyly. His shirt was already open. When she'd undone only one cuff button, chewing on her lower lip and sneaking little glances at his eyes, he knew this wasn't a good idea. He'd never last through another bath and have any stamina left to bathe her. "Let's bathe you first." His words were foggy and his breathing wasn't at all stable.

"Kiss me," she whispered, lifting her mouth.

She'd found something he knew how to do. And he hugged her bare breasts tightly against his hairy chest as he held her, feeling her with his body, his hands, his mouth. He kissed her very sweetly, but that didn't last. It wasn't any time at all until his kisses had turned sexual and hungry. Tense and urgent.

And his hands got out of hand as they scrubbed and squeezed and sought. He was embarrassed by his conduct, but not enough to stop. She didn't appear to notice that he was being really very forward and bold with her. She didn't slap at his hands or complain. She just wiggled and rubbed—she was rubbing herself against him!

By golly, no wonder those TV men sweat and concentrated and quit talking. So did Clayton. He sweat and concentrated and didn't say a word. He knew almost immediately that he would have to put on the condom. He wasn't going to be able to let her bathe

him again, not successfully. And he'd never in this
world last through giving her a bath.

So he got her out of the rest of her clothes and he
tore off his own, not waiting for any help. He held her
tightly, groaning with need. And she pawed at him and
made little sounds that about drove him crazy. Then
he picked up the packet.

What had Ruben Blades done? If Clayton recalled
correctly, Blades had pulled the banana free from the
bunch. Clayton looked at himself. He certainly wasn't
going to do that. Then he put the tips together and
began to carefully roll the condom on, leaving a little
extra at the tip.

Clayton's hands were trembling. He was sweating
with his passion, and he was embarrassed by his own
body, which had begun to lose a little starch. He half
turned away from Shelley, self-conscious and uncertain.

She was fascinated, and shifted so that she could
watch. She said, "Here. Let me hold these for you."
And she cupped him!

Startled, he shivered with the sensation and became rigid. He even blundered and had to start again
in donning the shield, but he did manage. He was very
ready and turned to her. "Oh, Shelley..."

She smiled at him and led him to the bed. And it was
easy. It was so natural and amazing. While they didn't
quite synchronize their movements, each was eagerly
helpful. They climaxed reasonably close, and it was
very satisfying, if somewhat disorganized.

Still with racing hearts and gasping breaths, he lifted
from her enough to look at her, and they both laughed
in their delight. It had been a rather crudely managed
romp.

He collapsed onto the bed and sighed with great satisfaction. He'd done it. She was amazing. No wonder there was so much about love on TV. It was a miracle.

He slept. And he assumed she did, too. But he awakened to find her watching him with a cream-fed smile. His funny bone tickled and he laughed. "Why do you smile that way, you wicked woman?"

"I think we'd better go into town."

"Why?" Why leave then?

"It isn't reusable." She shrugged her lax shoulder.

Straight to the point. "Come here and convince me."

They had a hard time getting dressed because they laughed and teased so much. He found he had a natural bend to that. And he was surprised. He'd never been teased by a woman.

His parents had had humor, and there'd been much laughter in the family. They had been cheerful people. But then when just his parents were together, they'd teased each other in the kindest and silliest ways. Clayton hadn't been a part of it. He only remembered the tone of his parents' soft, private laughter late at night or off in the woods together. That was how he and Shelley sounded now, and Clayton understood the difference in his parents' laughter. Besides being parents, they had been lovers.

This was being lovers. He took Shelley into his arms while she was still wiggling and teasing, and he just held her close. She must have recognized the difference, for she quietened. They stood that way for a while. Then Clayton kissed her with sweet gentleness, and she laid her head on his chest and held to him.

They did get organized. Then he drove the car. They went into town to replenish their supply and that night they made a dent in it. He was so greedy that he finally hesitated, but she encouraged him. She touched him until she found the places that made him groan, and she tickled little places that excited him. She suckled and licked and fingered, exploring him.

That excited his own adventuring on her. And he, too, explored, with awkward hands and mouth, nuzzling and touching. Pressing loving kisses, he smoothed excited flesh and crinkly hair as he made her known to his hands and body. Her breasts filled his hands, and he kneaded them with luxuriant sensuality. He moved her about and tried different ways of entering her willing body, and he loved her. He was a diligent learner.

It was dawn when she lay on her stomach with a knee bent and one foot in the air, playing with his beard. "I love having you suck at me and feel your beard around your mouth. It makes me want you."

He vowed, "I'll never shave again."

"Do you wear a beard because you want to look like a pirate?"

"No. It's to cover the scars."

"What scars?" She frowned.

"A cougar and I disagreed about a path. I hadn't known it was his path, and I had tried to go down it."

"Who won?"

"He did. He's endangered and I'm not. I had a hell of a time getting away. He was mad."

"Rabid?" she asked alarmed.

"No. Irritated."

She shook her head and had to laugh, but her hands were gentle on him.

He told her huskily, "You're a natural lover."

"How do you know that?"

"You must be," he said tenderly. "You've been so nice to me. You've let me love you so sweetly. I really like having you naked and willing. I can't believe I was ever without you."

She pouted. "Why didn't you call me when you were with the jumpers?"

"I've never had a telephone. I never think to use one. We have a radio for emergencies."

"Being that far away from me wasn't an emergency?"

"I ached for you," he groaned, holding her.

"Why didn't you tell me that?"

He pulled away, trying to see her eyes. "I came back, and you wouldn't even look at me."

She was indignant. "You didn't come near me. You just sat on that bedroll. I had to go to you and then you didn't even smile."

"I'd been on my feet for a couple of days." He smoothed her hair as an excuse to put his hand on her. "I hadn't slept in two days. I'd hitchhiked for almost twenty-four hours to get to you. You looked at everything but me."

"I was trying to get you to notice me."

He put his hands on her. "I sure as hell noticed you—from the first day when I got off that pickup at the meadow. You didn't even see me. I was a long time just getting you to say hello to me."

"I didn't know that you wanted me to do that," she complained.

"I wanted you."

She turned over onto her back and raised one knee as she put her hands up alongside her head. "You'll have to say 'Please,' and coax me."

He slid over on top of her and his body insidiously worked her knees apart. He lay on her with his weight on his forearms and he kissed along under her ear, his hot mouth in that curly beard giving her goose bumps. He moved down so that mouth was above her breasts and he rubbed his beard gently over her. He suckled on her sensitive flesh, his fevered mouth and scalding tongue working at her until she gasped with the sensation.

And he made love to her again. This time their bodies were in better sync, and their movements were voluptuous. There was no teasing or giggles. He shifted from her to free his hard hand and moved it, pressing and feeling along her woman's flesh. His fingers closed around her sensitized breast and puffed it so that the satin nipple was there for his tongue to lick and tease. Then his hand moved down to her stomach and pressed slow swirls there as he watched her eyes. She writhed as his bearded face gave its attention to her stomach and she began to make little urging sounds.

He slid those strong fingers into her blond fluff and petted her before he slid a finger farther and explored her readiness. She was a little tender from his night's attentions and flinched, so he kissed her and gave her his sympathy. He murmured soothing words to her and drove her crazy.

She insisted, and he demurred. She begged, and he said, "I've been too greedy." She had forgotten that it was he who was to say "please" and coax her.

So after she coaxed and pulled at him, he slid into her sheath and lay quietly while she felt him. He waited. He had had her enough, by then, so that he could lie still, sheathed by her.

But she was learning, too, so she tightened muscles and squeezed him. He gasped and covered her mouth to kiss her deeply. She moved sinuously beneath him, and he rode her movements in erotic pleasure. He moved in counterpoint with a swirl, and it was then she who gasped in pleasure.

And in their point and counterpoint, as in a duel, they both won.

When they finally arose and showered together, he couldn't not touch her. His touches weren't demanding or erotic. He petted her, touched her, felt her. Her lips were swollen from his kisses, and her eyes were dreamy. She tolerated his handling and she smiled. She was an erotic woman. How had he been so lucky to find her? To recognize, on sight, that it was she whom he wanted?

She did remember to call in the orders for supplies and to request the shower truck be refilled.

They had a meal. Was it breakfast? What had they eaten? He had no idea. Wolf had finished most of a rabbit and was lying by the pool, watching out over the countryside. He gave Clayton a tolerant look. The wolf knew he and Shelley were lovers. He could probably smell them on each other.

"Don't dress. Let me look at you," Clayton coaxed. "I've never gotten to watch a woman move, and you're so beautiful. Let me see you."

But Shelley found she couldn't walk around completely naked all day. It made her shy and self-conscious, so she pulled on a soft cotton blouse and long skirt but she wore no undergarments.

Clayton could put his hands on her through the material, and it was a sensation that was especially thrilling to him. She allowed it, her eyes amused and lazy on him. He would lift her skirt and enter her, not to make love but to experience the erotic fact of her.

He would lean, lift her breast to his mouth and suckle her through the thin material and that too was exciting to him, just to do that, to have the freedom of her. And it stirred him to see her pale nipple through the patch of wet left on the cloth by his mouth.

She would stretch and move her body, knowing that he watched, showing herself off to him. He saw that was so, and he smiled. His movements were easy and contented. He had found paradise.

She put on some sort of low-heeled slippers and, hand in hand, they moved out along the trail through her woods, along the gentle slope. The winds were from the northeast, clearing the smoke from that part of the sky, and it was cool out of the sun. He took off his shirt and put it on her, and she inhaled his clean scent.

Their day together was an orgy. They sated themselves. They never once denied their desire nor curbed it. They made love wherever they happened to be, as they found themselves in need and the wanting was soothed. They didn't always go to climax, but coupled just to do that, then parted to allow their fever to grow and be teased. They experimented and tempted. So in their private paradise, they were never beyond hand's reach.

He told her, "I like the way your breast tilts with this candy kiss perched up here this way." And he licked her nipple through the light cloth, squeezing her breast to hold it just so.

He told her, "You have the nicest bottom I've ever seen." And his hands squeezed the rounds as he kissed her. He explained, "I'm an expert. I've watched bottoms on TV. Especially on MTV."

"Ah." She slanted a chiding look at him.

He continued his dissertation. "Your waist is so tiny. See? I can almost put my hands clear around you. But I can't do that up here." He spread his hands on her breasts. "Or down here." His hands filled with other rounds.

She put her hands on him and said, "If I were playing baseball, I'd need another hand."

Having never played baseball, he didn't understand, so she showed him.

He waggled her head with one large hand, then smoothed her blond hair and played with it. Then he had her lean over so that he could see that her decorations matched.

She said she preferred his beard. She loved it. But she needed him to shave so that she could see if she liked his face. So he shaved, and she watched as he did that. His face hadn't had the needed stitches so the scars were puckered here and there. She had to sit on his lap as she examined him carefully, tilting his face. "You do look like a pirate." She kissed along the scars.

"Dishonest?" He frowned at her.

"Adventuresome."

He nodded with that and said, "I like the idea of the pillage-and-rape part."

"I feel I've been carried away into an adventure in my own house. I had no idea how exciting it could be to be with a man. I only knew that I wanted—"

"You hadn't...? I'm...? You never?"

"No." She shook her head slowly.

"You sure took to it. You didn't freeze up or cry or anything, like on TV. I thought maybe you'd done it with that..." He didn't finish. He wasn't going to name the doctor.

"That...what?" She was curious and encouraged a reply.

"I thought maybe you'd done it a time or two."

"No. I was never curious about any other man."

"I made you curious?" he asked. "That's all?"

"Right at first. I missed you so awfully when you were gone from the meadow."

"Why didn't you say so?"

She countered: "I let you do all sorts of things when you had me out in the woods."

"You didn't let me do this." He demonstrated.

"Well, that seemed awfully personal."

"But you let me do this." He stood her up and showed her all the things she had allowed.

"I couldn't have," she protested. "That's outrageous! I would never have allowed that."

"You had me on my ear." He made "ear" into three syllables.

"I'd have noticed."

Heartfelt, he assured her, "I sure noticed."

"And...did you like that? Doing that?"

"It's all that kept me going these last couple of weeks." He looked at her very possessively and kissed her sweetly. Then he set her from him, held her away, took a deep, steadying breath and said briskly, "We need to face the fact that your house could well be on a fire run. I don't think it could burn from the south, but the northwest wind could carry some live sparks that would act like a handful of matches. These trees are just as dry and just as easy to burn as the forests all around here. Tell me what you want to take down to the cave."

"To the cave?" She was still recovering from his shift of focus.

He nodded in agreement and finished her sentence: "While I can still walk." Then he elaborated: "We need to put aside enough so that you have something left if the fires come through here. Like half your bedding, half your rugs, half your dishes. That sort of thing. You need a starter set of things. What about your pictures?"

She looked around at the sand paintings. Those fragile works of art. "Yes. Some of the rugs. The pictures."

So he packed them, padding them with linens, and he began to carry them to the cave. Wolf was companionable and trotted along. It was a long walk, but Clayton felt the need to get it done.

Shelley helped, but she just wasn't used to that kind of work. She was a little disgruntled. "I believe this is silly."

"It could be," he admitted. "But why risk it? This is the worst drought in the history of this land."

"I think you're hyper."

"I hope so. But Shelley, I did this at my place, too."

"Okay. Okay. I give up."

He chose ways for her to rest. They took a flashlight and explored the cave for a way and noted that it had been used as a dwelling. It showed old marks of leveling on the floor and there were shards of fired clay. They speculated when that would have been. Later he asked her to make him a cake while he lugged more of her things down to the cave. She didn't have a cart or a dolly. It was all done on his back and in his arms.

She still scoffed.

But he was happier with even that much of her stuff down in the cave.

"Stuff?" she questioned his use of the word.

"Yeah."

"I've collected that...stuff very carefully, and I consider them treasures."

He shrugged. "One man's meat is another man's poison."

"It's a reach, but I understand."

"We gave up collecting things, to keep, a long time ago. And that's proven to be a blessing time and again."

"Then you aren't trying to collect me?" She gave him a very small smile, but it went with a very attentive look.

"I'm thinking on the risks."

She laughed in delight, then saw that he was serious.

Seven

———

Shelley was back on Clayton's lap, listening to him. Clayton had never talked so much in all his almost thirty years. She was such a listener, such a questioner, so curious that he poured out all his gathered thoughts, which he'd never before shared with anyone. "I tried to be like other men. I would go to Gasp and—"

"Gasp?"

"It's a little place that's closest to our mountains. There's a filling station, a general store and a café. It's a nice place. I'd watch the men who came in there. Truck drivers and tourists. One truck driver in particular. I heard Gasp was a regular stop for him. He'd wheel up in his orange pickup, come into the café and order five beers lined up. He just did that, and everybody laughed and seemed to like him."

"Not a six-pack?"

"No. He explained that he wasn't a boozer, he just drank five. He'd be loud and laugh loud, and everyone was tolerant of him. The waitress flirted with him, and he'd pat her backside. I would watch them. She'd go in his truck with him and not come back for a long time. And now I know what they did."

"What?" Her word was sly encouragement.

"Like us." His look was tender. "They'd made a lot of love in that long, long time they'd been gone. She'd come back sleepy, moving slow and smiling, and he'd drive off until the next time."

"And?" she coaxed.

"I tried it. I—"

"The *waitress*?" Shelley was indignant.

"No. No. Let me tell you. I went into the café one day, this was a couple of years ago, and I was loud and ordered five beers lined up, just like that other guy had done. And they looked at me cautiously and hesitated. I said to go *on* and *do* it. So they did. And I drank one down just the way that other guy had done.

"I felt a little peculiar. I don't know what happened but after the second one went down my gullet, I fell over backward and woke up much later, out in the back of the café, with one hell of a headache. I'd thrown up on the floor, and they were disgusted with me. They never let me order another beer. I'd never had one before and didn't know how to drink. But I can tell you this: Never drink two beers on an empty stomach." He was imparting hard-earned knowledge.

"Right."

"However, I did have to admire all the time that other guy had put in, learning to drink five beers and still navigate. That is a skill. But after that, I looked for other ways to make friends. I did try to pat the waitress on her backside, but she slapped me so hard that my head rang for two days."

Shelley nodded. "You need some preliminaries before patting women."

"I did realize that almost right after the ringing stopped," Clayton confided gravely. Then he shared another try to communicate with other people. "There was men who told jokes, but I had no store of tales. I tried, but I couldn't remember the punch lines.

"And there were people who talked about the news. I watched CNN, but the things that happened were so outside my life that I didn't relate to them. I know that's un-American, but it was the way I felt. You get that way, when you live in the mountains. Nothing seems to matter to you outside your own special place. And you do feel protected and above the rest of the country."

"Probably altitude sickness addled your wits," she suggested.

"That is possible," he conceded. "However, I have decided opinions on special things, but I admit to ignoring those that don't particularly interest me," he told her. Then he added rather pensively, "My mother had a strong opinion on everything. I believe my dad mostly opposed her opinions, but he was courteous about the opposition. Mother never would marry him. She was a hippie, you understand, and 'a piece of paper' didn't make a marriage. Dad finally had to adopt me to make me legal."

She was unperturbed by that, but asked, "Where are they?"

"They...died."

"They couldn't have been very old. What happened to them?"

"They... I don't know that I can talk about it."

"Tell me," she coaxed gently.

"They were... killed."

"My God. How? In a wreck?"

"No. Three men were hunting. And they ran across my mother. She was such a gentle woman. One pretended to be hurt. She believed in peace and love. So she was a sucker for an approach like that. She went to him, and they jumped her.

"They were on our land, trespassing. My dad heard them laughing, and he went to see what was going on. When the bastards looked up and saw him coming at them, they riddled him."

Clayton was silent for a while, his breath uneven. Finally he said in a low voice, "I looked for them. There were three. I saw their tracks. A Ranger had seen them too, but the trackers misled me with false directions. They got them. Mother had marked them well. But they swore they'd never seen 'the woman' and knew nothing about the man who was 'accidentally' shot. They claimed their scratches were from the brush when they were after a wounded deer. And while they admitted they had been in the forest that day, they swore they hadn't trespassed onto our land.

"They are wealthy and well-connected. No charges have been filed. The investigation is still going on. I have some of the bullets. They match their kind of guns. They say those guns were stolen. Those are the 'hunters' you hear about." His voice was cynical.

"Is this the 'risk' you are weighing?"

"Yes." His face was grim. "I can't have you involved with me, until this is settled."

"Don't you believe you're already 'involved' with me?"

"I mean . . . committed." He looked at her steadily.

"I'm not dallying," she warned him. "Have you noticed that you didn't have this attitude of not 'involving' me until after we'd been together?"

"If you think I'm going to be sorry for that, you're wrong. But I have been careful for you."

"Of my body," she corrected.

"Yes."

"What about the rest of me?" She was very serious. "What about how I feel? I care about you. I want to be with you."

And he asked her: "What would you do if this had happened to your parents?"

Shelley "saw" her gentle, timid parents murdered so carelessly. She looked at Clayton soberly, but she didn't reply.

"I have to catch them."

"It is the law to leave lawbreakers to the lawmen."

"But the courts can be influenced by technicalities. Because the long pharmaceutical name of a drug was slightly misspelled in a prosecutor's charge, a person got off. My parents were murdered over four years ago. They are dead, but the murderers still run free. They have lawyers arguing for them. My parents didn't have anybody arguing for their lives."

"I don't know the solution." Shelley shook her head in compassion. "Caging people to sit and wait for time to pass doesn't seem logical. We need a place to put people so that they can no longer be a threat to others. But this problem is everywhere. People don't feel safe in this country. My parents live in Bethesda,

Maryland, in a high-rise, and they don't have any idea what I'm doing, clear out here."

"How did you get . . . clear out here?"

"I saw a film on the West, and I was tired of gloomy, overcast skies. So I put in an application with a land developer, and I was hired. But when I realized that they were set on parceling off the land and cutting it all up, I resigned. I'm between jobs right now."

"How do you eat?" he asked with concern.

"I have an income."

He nodded, understanding that.

"Do you have any brothers or sisters?" she wanted to know.

"No. My hippie mother was of the zero-population conviction."

"Although my mother wasn't anywhere near to being a hippie, she too, was of that persuasion."

"Well, I am glad their only contribution was female."

"Me, too." She smiled a tiny bit and touched his cheek with gentle fingers.

Their regard became squishy in a way that would have made any observer groan in amused disgust. Then they kissed for a while before she told him, "I'm an environmentalist," as if confessing to something rather weighty.

"In these times, with all that's going on, you have to be." He was positive about that. "Do you know the government wants to bury stuff in New Mexico salt mines that will be very very hazardous for *two hundred fifty thousand* years? Just think of that! It boggles my mind."

Pensively, her head on his shoulder, she sighed and mourned, "At least you can't see it. You can here. The fires are ruining this land."

"Actually, no."

She roused and shifted to look at him. "No?"

"It does sound odd, but the fires are good for this land. Didn't you listen to Spears during orientation? After the winter comes, there will be a rejuvenation of the land. There'll be more varieties of plants. The ground isn't scorched deep, so the roots of the grasses are unharmed. Next spring the flowers will be spectacular."

"But what about the trees?"

"There'll be some loss. The aspen and maples. The fires burn their leaves and the next year's buds, but the roots aren't harmed. It'll take some time, but they'll mostly be okay. The pines have all those little spines around the bud ends of the branches. Fires burn off the outer ones, and the buds are mostly okay. I saw a demonstration on TV," he said in as aside.

"Of course," he continued, "nothing survives the fire storms. But even then, the ashes put new nutrients into the soil. Next spring will be beautiful. And in a couple of years, it will be amazing. That's because there's nothing poisonous in the natural fires, so nature can recover. It's the things man does that kill the land. There are still terrible scars out West where the miners scourged the earth looking for gold, laying waste to whole mountains, ripping away the topsoil that nature takes so long to make. I wonder if the land will ever recover."

Curious, she asked, "How do you make a living?"

"We have land. We . . . now it's just me. I allow the selective harvest of trees for wood products. I don't get as much for the wood, because it isn't as handy to go in and just take a couple of trees here and there. But they do it by helicopter and it works. I get the taxes paid and have a little left over." He looked at her to see if she was worried about him being able to support her.

"What if it all burns?"

He reassured her. "I'll help in replanting. I would still have the land."

"One mountain?"

He turned out his hands. "Several. And some meadows. It isn't straight up and down. I trap and hunt and fish. There's a fine trout run. Do you like trout?"

"Not especially."

"With lemon and wild onions?" He tempted. "Basted with butter?"

"Your own cow?"

He teased, "I milk buffalo."

"Do you really?" She made it appear she believed him; if he wanted to, he could.

He grinned. "No."

She felt she needed to mention it, so she said, "I don't especially like the idea of trapping animals."

He countered: "I don't especially like people to be hit by cars. It seems such a waste."

"Touché." Shelley bowed her head briefly to acknowledge that. "But how can you be an environmentalist and then turn around and trap animals?"

"Animals can overrun a place. They need to be monitored because when there's an exploding population of people, there isn't enough land for an expansion in the numbers of animals. The animals have less and less acreage. We're careful what we hunt. We aren't slaughterers. Food from hunting is very like ham, lamb and beef. You eat those meats and wear leather. What provides it?''

She nodded once in a kind of acknowledgment. "I do like bacon for breakfast, and in toasted BLT sandwiches. And I like leather."

"I like women in fur."

"Where do you see women wearing furs?" She wanted to know that and waited suspiciously.

"On TV."

"Do you watch a lot?"

"It's my link with civilization," Clayton explained. "That and the town of Gasp. I do learn more from TV than I ever learned in Gasp, except about not drinking two bottles of beer on an empty stomach. I learned that in Gasp."

"Do you want to stay in your mountains? Don't you want to live in a place where there are other people?"

"I don't know." Then he cautiously asked, "Could you . . . would you . . . would you like to see my mountain?"

"Yes. I am curious."

"How far can you walk at a time?"

"I've never measured." She shrugged. "I don't know how quickly you walk or how steep the land would be."

"We could take a tent and do it in sections."

"How far is it from Gasp?" She waited.

He'd never figured the distance. He guessed, "A day."

She repeated, wanting to know more precisely, "How far?"

"I don't think we ever measured it in miles. We just walked it."

"Did your mother mind living so isolated?"

"She helped my dad rebuild after the last fire went through there."

"When was that?"

"After my dad came back from Vietnam. I was a kid then."

"What a woman she must have been," Shelley exclaimed in respect.

"Yes."

"You must miss them terribly."

He was still for a minute, then he put her aside and rose.

"Clayton..."

"I'm okay. I just can't think about them so directly."

"I'm sorry."

"Think of something else to talk about right now." He asked it of her.

"Where did you find Wolf?"

He nodded, grateful. "His mother was shot. Not by me, I don't shoot wolves. I found her and her milk was heavy. I knew she had some young ones. So I hunted for them. Wolf was the survivor. It took a little doing to get him going again."

"He's magnificent," she commented. Then she asked, "Is he contented to just be your companion?"

"He's young," Clayton explained. "He'll make up his mind soon."

"And he'll leave?"

"Yes." The reply was that brief.

"That would be tough."

"It's happened before. I'll find another companion."

"Me?" she teased.

"I do have that one thing that I must do first. Then I'm going after you."

"Oh." She flirted a little. "So you intend to lure me?"

"I'm working on making you into a sex maniac." He was smug. "Then I'll teach you to catch trout and stretch skins."

"Ugh."

He tempted her. "I'll fly in toasted BLT sandwiches."

"Oh?"

"Peacock tongues?" he tempted.

"Whatever."

He smiled at his love. "I'll spoil you rotten."

She stretched and smiled at him.

"So," he said softly. "So you want to be spoiled?"

"I'm willing to try it for a while."

"I have a lynx skin that a man gave me for writing a letter. It would look great around your naked shoulders."

She laughed low and intimately, and his skin shivered deliciously everywhere on his body. She asked lazily, "Do you slow dance?"

"No."

"Why not?" she wanted to know.

"Dancing that time on the road was the first time I've ever danced."

"But you know music."

"My music is all for a crowd," he told her. "For people gathered to sing or dance the old square dances."

"One isn't. That one piece you played made everyone grieve."

"Yes," he agreed. "I was grieving for you."

"For *me*? I was right there! And after you played that sassy one, I boldly, scandalously went into the shower where you were stark, staring naked, to give you a towel and to get to kiss you."

His voice was husky as he coaxed her. "Why did you want to kiss me?"

"I'd missed you terribly."

"Why didn't you stick around? I was ready to back you against the wall and do all sorts of things to your helpless body."

"Oh?"

He smiled.

"Like . . . what?"

But he only adjusted her until she was sitting astraddle his lap, and then he showed her how to do it yet another way.

She was astounded and laughed, her head tilted up, her hair down her back in a spill that he could touch as he held her bottom and moved her to suit himself. Then he nuzzled her breasts and moved his hands here and there.

She mentioned: "For a man who hasn't been around civilized people, if I am to believe you, you are very innovative with a female body."

"You inspire me."

That only made her laugh again. It was such a delicious sound. He loved teasing her and surprising her and listening to her sighs and exclamations and the intimate way she laughed. He told her in a growly voice, "I only do all these things to you because I like the wicked way it makes you laugh."

That only made her laugh again.

They ate another meal, and he ate about half the cake. "I haven't had a cake like that in...a very long time."

"Do you like pie?" she queried. "I'm really better at pies. What's your favorite?"

"Lemon."

"Now, that does surprise me," she exclaimed. "I'd have bet good money on chocolate."

"Lemon."

"Okay, okay. A one-track mind!"

"You figured that out!" His smile was charming.

Charmed, she informed him. "In this last about thirty-six hours, I've noted one strong tendency."

"I've never heard it called 'tendency' before."

And she laughed.

He moved around slowly, putting dishes away and clearing things, as she made him a lemon pie.

With the avid edge of sexual hunger blunted, the bone weariness from the last session of fire fighting caught up with Clayton. He moved more slowly, then not at all. And he dozed standing on his feet.

"Come." She took his hand and led him into the bedroom. "You need to go back to bed," Shelley scolded.

His tired eyes glinted and he replied, "I'm scared to. There's something on this bed that attacks me every time I turn around, and it drains me of my life source."

"Hah!"

"It's true," he protested earnestly. "Someone climbs all over my frame and is *lascivious* with my body parts."

"How scandalous."

"That doesn't sound sincere," he chided. "Are...
you the one?"

"Of course not."

How could she look so innocent? He laughed. It
bubbled inside him, and he found it delightful to simply lie back and laugh. He hadn't laughed like that in
a long time.

She instructed primly, "You need to take off your
clothes—"

"I've heard that before!" he exclaimed. "You *are*
the one! I knew it!"

"Hush. I'm only trying to get you comfortable."

She worked at the licentious buttons, which lured
women's fingers. He lolled back and allowed it.
"Yeah. Another approach. I'm learning about voracious women. This is just another ploy."

"Ploy?" she questioned, working busily on his
clothing.

"Plot?"

"You use odd words here and there." She peeled off
his shirt.

"The particular words fit."

"Where do you find them?" She took off his boots
and began removing his socks.

"In books. The words say what I want to say."

"You'll have to stand up." She tugged.

He did that tiredly, yawning. "If you're planning to
take off my pants, let's figure out something else. I'm
dead."

That word slid a prickle up Shelley's back, and she
sent a sharp look at him. "Here, you do it."

"I'll take a...rain check. Is that right? When you
can't get something, and they give you a promissory
note? You can take off my pants another time."

"I'll do that. Well, go ahead. Do it."

"You promise not to peek?"

She laughed that low, wicked sound.

He reached out and touched her cheek with his finger. "Who could know that you'd be a sensuously triggered woman? I feel I opened a beautiful fragile box and found such a treasure that I don't want you out of my sight." He had unbuttoned and unzipped his trousers.

"Oh, Clayton."

"Just your humor makes you special," he told her. "You are a delight. And you have so many good qualities, I'm scared you'll find me lacking. Then to learn that you will invite me to you, I can hardly believe my fortune. You're not just toying with me, are you? I could die without you."

"I'm here," she said gently. "Go to sleep. You keep talking mushy like that and you'll never get any sleep. I'll start proving things."

"Now don't challenge me." He paused in pulling down his pants.

"I wasn't! I wasn't!" she protested in mock alarm.

"One look from you, and I'm ready."

"I've noticed. Sit down. Here. Let me help." She pulled the pants from his hard, muscular legs, shook them out, folded them and lay them on a chair. "Can you swing your feet up onto the bed?"

"I can do anything."

Her smile was especially tender. "I know. The iron man."

With effort, he swung his legs onto the bed. "Any time you need me, just call."

"I'll do that." She pulled the sheet and a light blanket up over him, her warrior, and she went quietly away.

He heard the door close and thought how wondrous it was to have a conversation. And he had done his share of the talking. He was aware of great contentment as he fell asleep. And he slept dreamlessly, as if nothing could happen in his newly found paradise.

When he wakened it was very dark. He could smell the faint odor of smoke and alarms rang in him. But it was a faint smell from a dead fire. The wind had shifted.

He felt so comfortable. He heard as she sighed. That startled him and his head turned quickly. It was *Shelley* there in his bed? A dream come true! Then he remembered, and why, and he smiled.

Being careful not to disturb her, he reached for a condom and even managed it in the pitch-dark. He was pleased with the ability. He lay back, moved carefully over to her and reached to gather her into his arms. She was naked. His grin widened. He moved his hand on her. Her breasts were soft. How strange such firm rounds could feel so soft in his big, hard hand. The nipples were satin with a delicacy that became puffed and luxuriant under his kneading and rubbing.

She sighed and stretched slowly, making purring sounds. And his hands stroked down her body, over her hip and around to other rounds. He slid his hand down the back of her thigh and lifted her knee onto his hip, before he touched her gently.

She whispered, "How do you know to do that?"

"It's what I want." And he pressed his great interest along her hot lure. "How can your body be so cool to my hands, while you're so hot there?"

"I don't know." She shook her head in the darkness. "You're hot everywhere. Your hands, your body, your mouth, and whatever it is that you're rubbing along me. You're like a firebrand."

"No. A firecracker, and I'm about to go off."

"Heavens to Betsy!" She pretended alarm. "Are you dangerous?"

"Very. You're about to be impaled."

"Oh."

He rolled them over so that she was under him, and he breathed, "Now." And he slid into her sheath with newly acquired smoothness.

"You do that very well."

"I need more practice." He disparaged any skill. "There was an awkwardness, if you'd been paying closer attention and not trying to go back to sleep."

"You have my attention."

"Oh?" He couldn't think how to go on with his teasing, but he wanted to. He loved her sassiness.

She explained, "I knew what you were doing when you got up for the condom."

"You could have helped." Now that was pretty quick.

"I thought it was good practice for you to do it alone and not have me helping all the time."

"Helping?" His tone was puzzled.

"You've never noticed that I've had to hold you?"

Huskily he encouraged, "Where did you hold me?"

But she had to squirm and reach up under her thigh until she could cup him and show him what a help she could be.

He made a strangled sound and said gruffly, "Ohh," on an intaken breath.

"See?" She was sassy. "I've had to help you every single time, just that way. It's rather sad that you can get along now without my help."

"I wanted to surprise you."

In a lovely throaty way, she told him, "I like surprises." And she squeezed him.

Again...

And again...

Eight

The lovers' idyll lasted another two days. Clayton's lemon pie was eaten, then a chocolate one, since that was Shelley's favorite. And they talked more easily. More seriously. They learned more about what they thought and how they felt about life.

Clayton asked, "How did you decide to leave home? I never did."

And Shelley replied, "I didn't have your adjustment to my environment. I was restless in the city. My parents are contented with a placid life of routines. They go to a play or a museum. They attend church each Sunday. There isn't ever any interruption or something done by impulse."

"You must have puzzled them." She puzzled him, and he'd just met her.

She shrugged. "I would try to talk to them, to find out how they felt about events, but they would reply,

'It will be solved,' as if they had nothing to do with our country.''

''What did they do in the sixties? In that fermented time?''

'' 'Fermented.' '' She tasted the word. ''That's an excellent way of describing what it must have been. They said people were stirred up and the artwork was chaotic—''

''That's all?''

''—and the music was loud. They mentioned the love-ins and communes. They thought *Hair* was immodest, and they mentioned the personal misconduct in a hushed, vague way. They are fortunate they believe alike. Your parents were such opposites that I wonder how they managed?''

''We-l-l-l-l...'' He drew out the word as his mind went back to judge them freely for the first time. ''For one thing, Dad kept her out here as the earth child she claimed to be. And for another, they loved each other very much. I believe their relationship was one of great love and great tolerance for each other. With him so conservative and her so liberal, they would have made a great study for statisticians. In their case, opposites did attract. I'm a lot like my mother.''

That made Shelley bite her lip to stop an exclamation and she had to look off to the side.

He concluded, ''I like living in the woods.''

She had to point it out: ''Apparently so did your conservative father.''

''That's true,'' Clayton agreed. ''But he wasn't anything like my mother. He believed in the laws and never questioned any of them. And he admired politicians, while their conduct made my mother pull her hair. They made very interesting pro-and-con debates for a child of theirs."

"And you really believe you're a flower child?" She did question such an assertion.

He agreed: "A male version."

"How do you feel about equal rights for women?"

"A man can take care of his woman."

"What about a woman who has no man?"

A simple solution for him. "She ought to find one."

"If there aren't any?"

"She could live in a commune and share," he suggested.

"Should I do that?"

"No."

"I can see that you're a true liberal."

He added: "You have to know that I'm not so strong about other things that are very liberal."

"I hesitate to inquire what those might be."

He filled it in. "I believe in a day's work for a day's pay. And that the government isn't there to raise people's kids. I believe that people ought to be responsible for themselves."

"And you see that as being...liberal?"

"I don't believe in the government interfering with our lives. They're there to do what we want. They're our elected *representatives* and not our keepers. They need to keep out of things."

"Very liberal." She was being snide.

"Well, there might be a few tinges of conservativeness. I got some of Dad's genes, too."

"I would love to've known your mother."

He didn't reply for several minutes. When he spoke, his voice wavered and his words were slowly spoken. "She was really something. But then, so was my dad.

The only time I saw him out of control was when she died. Dad charged those men unarmed. I was too far away to help. I—'' Clayton's voice broke.

Shelley put her arms around Clayton, and he cried for the first time in all the years of his terrible grief. He did it so poorly that Shelley wondered if he'd ever cried before.

When the sweep of emotion passed, Clayton, this flower-child liberal, was embarrassed by his conduct and was silent. She had the gall to ask, "Are you embarrassed because you cried?"

He couldn't believe she'd say it right out loud that way, and couldn't look at her as indignation touched him.

She went on: "You would be a stone if something that terrible didn't force your emotions. If you could take that like a stoic, I'd not be able to love you."

He glanced obliquely at Shelley, testing her candor. Then his mind sorted her words. "You love me?"

She sighed with surrender. "I believe I do."

"Don't get serious on me until I'm free. You know what I have to do."

She allowed: "You may try to capture them, but you must promise to turn them over to the police. I'll give you a year."

"Are you laying out rules?" he asked soberly.

"You do it easily enough, and it's a free country. I can do what you can."

He was silent, regarding her, while she looked off and back to him in quick glances. Her chin was up as she waited for his reply. But after a time, his eyes glinted and a little smile flicked along his mouth. "You can do anything I do?"

She lifted her chin impudently. "Or it's counter-point."

And he laughed. It was a bit watery, but it was a real laugh.

She smiled at him. "You're a very special man. Would you please play the courting song for me?"

"Are you courting me?"

She sighed in an exaggeratedly disgusted way. "If you haven't figured that out by now, your parents would *blush* for their stupid son, Clayton."

Even as off-kilter as his emotions had just been concerning his parents, Clayton had a fleeting picture of them shaking their heads at him; and he had to slowly shake his own head as he smiled at his love.

So he took his fiddle outside and played that sassy courting song he'd performed at the meadow. And this time, fully concentrated on the sounds within the music, Shelley laughed in delight.

Over by the pool, Wolf sighed in boredom.

The fires began to crowd the inhabited places. And the fire fighters were called upon to put in longer hours. Clayton's leave wasn't up, but he returned to the lines, leaving Wolf to guard Shelley.

To leave her was like leaving Shangri-la. He expected to begin deteriorating as he traveled farther away from her. She was his life. That thought troubled him. He really loved her? Or was it just that he wanted to be back in her bed? What sort of love did he have for her?

He thought about all the kinds of women he'd witnessed in Shelley. Her face with all its moods and expressions flickered through his mind like a slide projector on rapid. She wasn't at all ordinary. How could she be the kind of woman she was, with the parents she'd described? She was certainly special. And he knew his feelings for her were more than sexual. Much more. It was love. And it seemed like the kind his parents had had.

Clayton was now one of the old-timers among the fire fighters, and he was second-in-command under Juan Gomez. They had a team of raw volunteers who were just finishing orientation. They were sent to a small settlement of several houses. The people didn't want to leave their homes and had to be convinced. Coaxed. Argued with. Coerced.

Pets disappeared, and people got frantic. "I can't leave until we find Earl." Take on a pet, and you're responsible. They were good people, but they'd trade their lives for a dog?

One woman asked with strained exasperation, "How can I get a very pregnant cat into a motel with us?"

The rangers were magnificently patient and polite. There must have been some who became testy, but Clayton didn't hear of a one.

However, the volunteer fire fighters could be a little pushier. "Look. I've got my own place to worry about. Don't irritate me."

Did that move them? No. They asked with concern, "Where's your place?"

They retorted: "Move!" "Git!" "You're risking us, too. Get the hell out of here!"

The wind picked up and immeasurably complicated the whole people/property disaster.

How many times did they hear, "It's no use. Save the houses if you can, but we'll have to hope the road stops it."

They pinned their hopes on a road, a gully, or a stream or some other natural barrier. Sometimes the fires were stopped that way; sometimes they weren't.

But the unity among the fighters was remarkable. A common cause united the most diverse personalities. Arbitrary, arrogant people took directions from pipsqueaks they'd never have even noticed at any other time. They all really worked hard.

A light rain went through, giving them all hope, but it wasn't enough. It only cooled the air and slowed the fires fractionally. They needed more rain. Or snow. It wouldn't be unheard of to have snow, at that time of the year in that area. Without the fires, it was quite cool.

It was the middle of September by then, and Clayton and Shelley met briefly to reach their hands for the other's and to kiss softly. It was oddly gallant. It was a relief to see one another so briefly, to know the other was real and there.

Clayton helped the crew. There was again the problem of blisters suffered by the amateurs. The blisters were of one kind and sometimes of another. The fires were hot and popping. Occasionally an ember would fly among the line of workers. One woman was almost hit by a falling tree, but her male buddy pulled her aside at the last minute. Then the rescuer got mad because he had been so scared.

"You saved my life!" The rescued one was amazed.

"You damned fool!"

"I could've been squashed!" she exclaimed.

"Couldn't you hear it cracking?" he snarled.

She protested, "I thought the fire was just closer."

"God, but you're dumb."

"Thanks for saving my neck."

"Don't do that again," he begged. "I'd have a heart attack."

And they hugged each other.

So close friendships and companionships and care bloomed among the crews. And lovers happened. Clayton and Shelley weren't the only ones. The crew spent one frantic night looking for a pair, trying to remember when they'd last been seen. The searchers were scared spitless over what might have happened to them ... to find them aside in the forest, in a shared sleeping bag, blissfully asleep.

They'd dumped a bucket of water over the pair.

He'd protested, "How could we tell you we were sneaking off together?"

"You could've told *somebody*, so we wouldn't've worried."

"You're a bunch of mother hens," the male half groused.

"We were scared."

"Thanks. We do appreciate you worrying. We're sorry."

"I've got gray hair from all this." Clayton scratched his growing beard.

"It's just soot." Someone soothed him. "Take a bath."

And Clayton called to the skies, "Shelley!"

Everyone knew Clayton and Shelley were a couple, even Michael Johnson and Maggie Franklin. And Clayton said to Michael, "I'm glad Maggie has distracted you from Shelley."

"How do you mesmerize two women at the same time?"

"Shelley is supposed to be taken with me," Clayton told Michael. "Maggie isn't. She's just making you worry because you liked Shelley first, before her. Pay attention to Maggie and when you talk to her, compare Shelley unfavorably with Maggie."

Michael smiled in real humor. "Do you really think I can do that?"

"If you love Maggie, then you can." Clayton pronounced that. "I think if I hadn't seen Shelley, Maggie would've been the one. She's a gemstone."

Michael contemplated Clayton and said, "So are you. A little rough yet, but Shelley will polish you."

Clayton told the doctor earnestly, "If you realized it, Shelley was never for you. You're too conservative. She needed me."

"A wild man." Michael's tone was a little snide.

"A free man." Clayton corrected. "The son of a flower child."

"Your mother was a ... hippie?"

"One of the best," Clayton replied with sober respect.

"You're too old to be a hippie's child. You're almost thirty."

"She was marching with Dr. Spock and taking part in the Vietnam protest before it became a national movement." But Clayton wasn't there to talk about his mother. He explained to Michael, "Maggie is just right for you, and she'll understand your stodginess."

Unbelieving, Michael echoed, "Stodg-i-ness?" And the last two syllables sent his voice up almost a whole octave.

"You can't help it, you probably had normal parents," Clayton comforted the man who might still become another friend. "Pay attention to Maggie."

Michael grumped: "She watches you."

With his newly acquired expertise in women, Clayton assured the neophyte, "She's trying to make you notice her." Adding research done for his "graduate degree" as a television viewer. He advised, "Take her home and take her to bed. Convince her." That last had a nice ring to it, and Clayton smiled.

With a roughened voice, Michael demanded, "Is that how you convinced Shelley?"

"Careful." Clayton's growled, mild word was very threatening.

One of the rangers came along and mentioned, "You know that trio we've been watching for you?"

"You are?" Clayton hadn't known.

"They've been around in a black pickup."

Carefully Clayton asked, "Helping?"

"Shooting 'stamping wild animals.' The other day someone reported that anonymously, but gave no directions. He said that he'd seen them hauling away a bison."

"Nobody stopped them?"

The ranger sighed and squinched his face up disgustedly. "The fires have been distracting."

Clayton's mouth became stubborn. "Maybe they'll be back."

"Leave it to us. I only mentioned it because you tend to believe you're in this all alone. We knew your parents for a long time. *And* you. We're going to get them. Watch and see."

"If it's possible, I want to be in on it."

"Best not." The ranger shook his head.

"Look, sir—"

"Hell, I wish I hadn't said anything."

"No," Clayton said. "I appreciate your telling me."

"Keep your nose clean."

Clayton watched the ranger walk away and the thought came that people had known his parents, and him. He'd never paid that any attention. He supposed they would have known his dad, with the Masterson family being there so long. Some of the Masterson land had gone into the western edge of Yellowstone National Park. But it was good to know somebody else believed those men had been the murderers.

Shelley came to Clayton, and they stood quietly, holding hands. Wolf came over and leaned against Clayton's leg in a lonesome way. Clayton held his love's hand and his other hand rubbed the wolf's head.

Clayton was very tired and very dirty. She told him softly, "You look as if you need a nice bath."

He smiled. "Yeah? There're only showers here."

"I know where there's a tub that isn't being used—and I need to check on my house." She flirted a glance.

"Well, I could go along and ride shotgun."

"How kind you are."

He grinned. "I'm always glad to oblige a lady."

"How about a sex maniac?"

"My shots have been successful? You've—" he sought the word "—evolved?"

And she laughed just for his ears and in such a naughty way that he was ready to test the premise. He told her, "You know I'm in charge of these people? And we have to move them to another place. This meadow is getting too much traffic, and the air is thicker with the smoke. The fires could be coming this way."

"When does your group move?" she asked.

"Right away."

"Where?"

He showed her on the map. The new location was a retreating one and would be south of her place. He told her, "I'll be able to catch a ride okay. Don't worry about me. You do have an alarm clock? I'm still not used to them. Do you know how to set it?"

She said, "Yes. When do you have to get back?"

"Don't you meet the food truck here?"

"I'm on rest," she explained.

"Then I'll find a way," he promised. "Don't worry about that, at all."

They kissed very gently, just touching lips, but they smiled into each other's eyes and were reluctant to let go of each other's hand.

It was almost dark when Clayton was free of duties. He checked out with Juan Gomez, and he borrowed a truck from one of the men.

"Take care of it," the loaner cautioned.

"Want me to ask somebody else?" Clayton smiled a little, and assured the loaner honestly, "I've never wrecked a car or truck yet. Not even a dent." He'd only been driving for a month.

So he found himself on his way to Shelley's to spend the night with her. He wished he wasn't quite so tired. He smiled. He wasn't *that* tired.

She came out of her house into the early dusk, and even in the September chill she was wearing only that soft cotton blouse and skirt. She was silhouetted against the doorway of her house so he saw that she wore nothing else.

He wasn't half as tired as he'd thought. But he got out of the truck slowly. And when they met, he took the kiss she offered him, but he said, "You ought to know who's here before you open your door."

"I knew it was you."

"No." He was stern. "You don't know this truck."

"It's been parked along the road since this new bunch started with you. I've seen it several times a day. You underestimate me."

"The guy who owns that truck wasn't the one driving it."

She nodded. "You've made your point."

He put his big hand on her bottom and pulled her close against him. "There's another point I'd like to make."

"Oh?"

"I need to clean up a little so you don't throw up from my smell when I take off my clothes."

"Umm," she said. "I believe I can help in that."

He lifted his brows to show that he was willing to consider almost any suggestion, no matter how silly it might be.

"I would rather you left your clothes out here, somehow, and I know I could sound finicky, but I would rather not have those things in my house. I'd have to fumigate."

"A very picky woman." He began to peel off layers. "Any way we can get these clean?"

"I discussed just that problem with my washer," she declared. "It has bravely volunteered."

"Good."

"I'm glad you're not depending on me, a rock and a beating board on the river to get that hooded jacket clean. The others don't get nearly as dirty as you."

He moved a placating hand. "They're too new at this, so we have to move around more to watch them."

"I think you attract dirt."

"Yeah."

"You have a beautiful body." She gave him a simple look of appreciation.

"Oh? It's not at all like yours. If I'm going to be an exhibitionist, then you ought to take your clothes off and help me feel comfortable, naked like this."

She could understand that thinking. "I suppose that would be the courteous thing to do."

He backed away to get a fuller view and get downwind, for her sake. Then he became aware of the pool, sitting there, full of cold water and idle. He smiled.

She didn't take any time at all to remove the flimsy garments, and he told her, "You're much nicer to see. Look at you. So sweet and very beautiful. I would like to kiss you. And I will in just a minute."

He went into the pool in a great splash, sending water everywhere. He surfaced and whooshed, making a walrus sound with his breath expelled in a head sweep, with his mouth just below the surface. Then he hung in the water, waiting to see what she would do.

She slid into that cold water in a beautiful dive, with only a few droplets of misplaced water. She came up near him, and they played like otters.

How amazing to have been that tired, and to have a cold swim revive him. He caught her every time, and she had to forfeit progressively more intimate favors. He lifted her from the pool with no effort, and pulled himself out with a great deal of water falling from him. He picked up a slippery wet Shelley and carried her into her house. There he dried himself while he looked at her.

He dried her very differently. He rubbed her hair with a fresh towel and used her dryer on it. Then he directed the warm air along his own hairy chest and under his arms. He sought and discovered other hair as he dried his legs and around his sex.

He turned his courteous attention to her. His big hand felt along her smooth legs, with the blower still on. He lifted her arm where there was none, and he kissed her there. He discovered a patch that was already dried, but he fluffed it and allowed the blower to seek out an errant droplet.

She said, "I'm about to go wild."

"Why?" He looked up from where he squatted at her side, and his face was so innocently curious.

"I believe you've delayed as long as you can." She sounded pretty sure.

"I'm enjoying this adventure."

"I have another aspect of it that you might find...entertaining."

"Yeah? What?" He rose effortlessly to his feet and looked down at her. "Do I watch or can I play, too? What's it called?"

"Uhh. Connections."

And he laughed.

During that night they played the game several times. It was entertaining, and he did enjoy doing it. Very much. He loved her. He held her to his body and he purred.

"Wolves don't purr." She scoffed.

"We had cats. They didn't stay around long. But we had them all through the years. And I liked hearing them purr."

"I like hearing you purr." She put her hands to his head and kissed his mouth very gently.

He told her, "You are my love."

With great sentiment she asked, "How did I ever find you?"

"Your spirit called to mine. I knew it was time to come looking for you, so I did."

"Do you believe that?" she asked gently.

"Yeah."

"And you'll give up the hunt for those murderers?"

"I think that will soon be solved."

She stiffened. "What do you mean?"

"They've been seen."

She popped up, sitting upright on the bed, in the dark room, and she said tersely, "You are not to be involved. I command you!"

"Cool down, honey, I never said I would be."

"Then tell me that you will not."

"I—I can't."

"Either you let the rangers handle this, or we are through! Do you understand? I mean it."

"Shelley. They were my parents."

"I understand that, but—"

He interrupted: "We'll talk about this another time. It's just about time to leave you here. Kiss me sweetly."

"Promise me, Clayton. I want your solemn promise."

"I can't give it."

"Then don't come back."

He sat silently for a long time. Then he said to his love, "I'll be back. You love me as much as I love you. This matter is something on the outside of the rest of our lives. The love is something we share. The other has nothing to do with us."

"It does."

He leaned over and kissed her cold cheek, then lifted her cold hand and kissed the palm. "I'll be back." And he left her bed.

She began to cry.

He turned back and held her cold body close to his heat. "You don't understand. It's what I have to do. When that's done, I'll come for you."

"I won't be here."

"Yes, you will. You love me."

He left her and dressed in his clean clothing from her dryer, then he stood in the door of her dark and silent room. "Take care of yourself," he told her. "I'll be back."

And she tore herself from the bed and flung herself into his arms where she wept stormily. And he held her, smoothing her hair gently and saying soothing things. But he left without the promise she again pleaded to hear.

The wind had risen. Hearing the sound of it singing in the tops of the trees, everyone groaned. The smoke was blown, and they all knew the wind would be carrying embers into new trees.

"Be calm," Juan told the untried crew. "Move deliberately. Pace yourselves. You have time. You can't get all excited or you might make a mistake. Think of your next move. Be organized. Your life could depend on it. When we get to the line, work at a normal pace. Slow and steady wins this race with fire, too. You know that. Listen to me."

And as they rode to the fires, Juan talked to the sober crew. And he did calm them. He made them appreciate the magnitude of the whole picture. And that each was to do only a share. "It isn't all in your lap.

You are a part of a great offensive. All that you have
to do is keep whole what houses and buildings we can
save. The land will be okay."

The crew was assigned to an area off the right fork
of an isolated road. The right fork was forest, and they
were put to working a firebreak to protect the road.
Then they had moved to the other side of the road to
begin another firebreak, just in case.

Juan's hand radio went out, and he asked Clayton
to go barricade the road and report it to headquarters.

Clayton took a woman from the line to block the
road with orange bedpacks so that no one would come
down the right-hand fork. The road was narrow and
it would be difficult to turn around if the fire leaped
the road. She helped with the barricade, then she returned to the line.

Clayton went to the communication truck parked
behind the school bus used to transport the crew. He
was to call in, but saw a ranger's car approaching. The
car slowed and stopped alongside Clayton. "Why is
the right fork closed?"

"We may lose the road if the fire jumps it. It's really
wild."

The ranger smiled. "That might simplify things
considerably. Have you seen—oh, is that you, Masterson?"

"Yeah," admitted Clayton. "What's the trouble?"

"Uh. Nothing. It's just that we're looking for...a
black pickup. Have you seen one?"

Clayton breathed almost to himself, "So they did
come back."

"You know?"

"Yeah." Clayton's voice became urgent. "Listen, I've got to stay here for now, with these kids. We need a radio. Juan's is out. And can you get Spears to send somebody up here to relieve me? I want to be in on... *it*."

"I'll see. Keep your eyes peeled. And Masterson, if you do spot them, call in. Don't go after them by yourself. Do you hear me?"

"Yes, sir. I hear."

"Then see to it that you listen and don't go off half-cocked. You know damned good and well that we've been watching that bunch all this time, even before they ever ran into your mother and dad. We know them. They wouldn't hesitate to whack you over the head and throw you into one of the fires. You know that. You know what they're capable of doing. Leave them to us. Hear me?"

"I hear." Clayton intoned the words.

"That isn't the answer I want."

"I'll... call in if I see them."

"Swear to me, Clayton. Otherwise I'll have to stay here with you and there'll be one less man looking. Swear."

"I swear I'll call in if I see them."

"And stay put." The ranger pushed it.

"Good luck."

"You didn't answer me. Are you going to stay put?"

Clayton explained, "I'm helping Juan Gomez with this bunch of greenhorns. I'm obligated to stay, you know that. Please. Listen to me. Contact Spears and get a replacement for me so that I can just go along. You have to know what this means to me. You must have seen my mother and what was left of my dad, or you've heard what it was like. You must understand that I have to be there.''

"God, man, sure I do. But *we* have to protect you! Let us handle it.''

"If they try to get away—'' Clayton was anguished.

"Trust us. We can haul them in on the bison alone. The guy that called in sent us pictures. We've got them nailed on it. Now we have a toehold. For your own good, stay out of this.''

Nine

How familiar are you with this particular section of the countryside?" the ranger asked Clayton.

"I've got a map." Clayton took it from his pocket and spread it out.

"We're here." The ranger pointed to the road. "As you can see, if they went down the right fork, the 'hunters' could just disappear. The left fork goes right back to the main road. There's no getting off it. It's either turn around and come back, or keep going. So if they should come this way, and the fire had blocked the right fork, they can only go on the left one, and they'll drive right into our welcoming arms." He studied Clayton for a calm minute. Then he said firmly, "If they come this way, let them come to us."

Clayton avoided a reply. "There aren't too many choices in roads. They could well come along this one."

"Do I have to stay here with you?"

"No, you go along. I'll send them your way."

"Tell me that you're staying neutral. I'll contact Spears, and we'll take you out of here." When Clayton was silent, the ranger said, "I don't trust you to wait for us. You can't do it alone. I'll be back shortly."

"Don't forget Juan's radio went out." Clayton added, "See if you can get us a replacement, will you?"

"Sure."

Clayton stepped back and watched as the ranger took the left fork and disappeared.

One of the crew, Jim, jogged up to tell Clayton, "Juan says he thinks it's going to jump. The wind's gusting. He said to call in and tell them that he doesn't think the road'll stop it."

"Right." Clayton went to the truck and radioed in. He put the mike back on its hook and said, "They just told me that they're soaking the houses below here. If it does jump, they'll have to tell the people to evacuate. Let's go."

"We don't appear to win very much." Jim was discouraged.

"Don't think that way." Clayton was positive. "We've done our damnedest. Nobody can ask any more than that. So we have won. We've lost some houses, but we've saved most of them, so far."

"It's really strange." Jim pointed down the right fork. "Look. That fire is so close, and there's no smoke right here. Look at the sun. It's so bright and clear."

"The wind's keeping the smoke low, but that means the embers and sparks aren't flying. That's pretty good. When those fly high, the new fires start acres away."

"Clay!" Another member of the crew, Otis, came running up the road. "It's jumped the road! Juan's pulled them back to a grassy space between the roads and they're working on the second back fire."

Clayton called out, "I'll be right there."

As he looked back up the right fork, Otis fretted, "The winds are so chancy, Clay, I think it'll storm the fire."

Clayton ordered quickly, "Here, you report it. I'll go— Who the hell's that?"

The pickup came barreling down the road, its heavy motor oddly loud above the roaring fire. Clay ran across the road and waved the orange flag for them to take the left fork. And the truck slowed somewhat.

Then in the slow motion of amazing occurrences, Clayton saw all three of the murderers were in that black truck. On the truck bed there were at least five magnificent pronghorn antelope stacked up.

Clay froze.

Then still in that same oddly quiet vacuum, Clay watched as the men stared at him, and he saw recognition come into their eyes. They knew him.

The exchange of that knowledge was like a bond between Clayton and the three in the truck. It stretched there, keeping them immobile for endless seconds.

They were where Clayton Masterson could reach them. Their expressions were briefly almost afraid. Their mouths opened in their shock. The truck clashed gears as it surged forward.

Had he only wanted revenge, all Clayton needed to do was to wave them into the right fork and the inferno would finish them. As fast as the pickup was being driven, the murderers, running from the rangers, would be around the bend and into the fire before they knew what was happening, and they would be burned alive.

But Clayton couldn't do it.

Just as Clayton signaled for them to take the left fork, their faces distorted. Through the glass windshield and windows, they snarled in vicious silence. The driver turned the pickup toward Clayton and tried to hit him, but Clayton jumped out of the way into the ditch.

And they took the right fork.

Clayton yelled, "No!" Getting up from the ditch where he'd fallen and running after the truck, he waved the orange warning flag, yelling "Stop!"

But the black pickup went faster. It roared through the contrived orange bedpack barricade and hurtled down the right fork toward the bend.

Otis yelled, "What's wrong with them? They did that deliberately! My God! They'll be fried!"

Clayton ran for the truck parked behind the school bus. He yelled at the two men, "Hurry! I want them alive!"

The other two got into the truck. Otis immediately called in to report, as Clayton started the engine and jerked the truck around the bus to follow.

Otis was saying, "A black pickup ran Clay off the road and went through the barricade up the right fork. The fire's jumped the road just around the bend, and they'll be in the middle of it before they realize what they're into. We're following."

The calm voice of the ranger said, "Did Clayton shoot at them?"

"What!" Otis yelled impatiently, "What sort of silly question is that? This is serious! Three guys are in a pickup, and they have about five pronghorns in the back end. Clay told them to take the left fork, but they tried to hit him as they went past, and they went through the barricade on the right fork. Listen to me! The fire jumped the road and those men will be fried by now. The winds are swirling and it could turn into a fire storm. Are you paying attention?"

"We're coming," the calm voice responded.

Otis hung up the mike and said in exasperation, "Did you hear that? 'Did Clayton shoot at them?' What a time to be funny."

Clayton said, "He was serious."

Otis stopped talking and leaned forward so that he could look around Jim in order to see Clayton's face. "Serious? Cut it out."

"Those men murdered my parents over four years ago, and I want them."

"But you told them to go down the left fork." Otis was uncertain.

"That wasn't planned, I just did it. If they're alive up there, I want them."

The three were silent as they sped up the right fork.

They hadn't even gotten to the bend when the explosion blew a high billowing fireball.

"Well," said Otis. "I guess we don't have to help you, after all."

Clayton had stopped the truck and was staring through the windshield when the shock wave rocked the car. But he dragged his stare from the higher flames and looked over at Otis. "You meant to help me?" The loner was startled by Otis's unsolicited loyalty. "You're crazy. You can't get involved in anything like that just on a man's say-so."

Otis shrugged. "They're dead." He punched the button, identified himself and relayed the information that the pickup had exploded.

"Any survivors?"

"We'll see. Very doubtful."

In some amazement, Jim spoke as if thinking aloud, "This has all been an incredible experience. I wonder what I would have done if the fire hadn't gotten them. I suppose I'd have pitched in—to even it up, you know. Three of them and three of us—"

Clayton interrupted. "I couldn't have allowed that. Jim, take the truck back to the bus, away from here. This is too close. The explosion has complicated the fire. We've got to help Juan."

Clayton and Otis left the truck. Jim turned with exceptional skill and drove back while the two jogged off the road, through the underbrush and finally contacted the crew. They were working furiously at the back fire, and Juan signaled for the two to help and where.

With their unique tools, they dug and chopped along to stop the controlled back fire. A frantic effort. So it was some long hours before they ever could stop and watch. The winds gentled, the fire paused. It softly met the back fire to kiss in flames and rest, flickering, sighing, seemingly contented.

The members of the crew were still stunned from the explosion they'd witnessed. Then they began almost to babble to Clayton, Otis and Jim, who hadn't been with them at the time. They needed to talk.

"The bullets!"

"Like firecrackers—"

"We all hit the dirt—"

"Some fool—"

"Did you see—"

Clayton was terse: "Any survivors?"

"A couple of 'em got out just before—"

"But they weren't far enough away and—"

"There were antelope on the back, and they went up in the air like they was alive and leaping when—"

"Nobody could've made it," yet another added.

Tense, Clayton urged, "Are you sure?"

"Look for yourself. It was a fire storm back there. Nothing can stand something like that. They've been cremated."

"Why were they on the road? You were supposed to barricade it," Juan said sternly.

"I did. They went over the barricade."

"Who were they?" someone asked. "Anybody know them?"

"They murdered my parents over four years ago."

There was a chorus of exclaiming: "What!"

"What is this?" Juan asked carefully.

"It's a long story."

"Did you misdirect them?" Juan asked.

Otis interrupted, very perturbed. "Jim and I was *there*. Clay tried to get them to go down the left fork. He really did! We saw him. They drove right over the orange packs, but before that they tried to run over *Clay*!"

But Juan was troubled. "There will be an inquiry."

Otis shook his head. "It was them that did it to theirselves. We was there, Jim and me. Clay did the best he could to keep them from the right fork. That's the truth."

Clayton said calmly, "I wanted them."

In the silence, someone asked, "What're you saying?"

"They killed my parents."

There was a stunned silence. Otis asked, "They did that?"

"Yes."

Juan said, "Holy Mother."

Otis hit his hand into his fist. "We shoulda had 'em. Damn!"

Clayton was anguished. "What in God's name made me wave them to the left fork when I *knew* this would happen if they took the right one? I tried to *prevent* their getting killed!" The thought appalled him.

"I guess you just solved it yourself," Jim supplied.

"How?" Clayton wanted to know.

"You said 'in God's name' and He probably just saved your hide and ours, too. Otis and I, we'd have jumped in. We'd probably be dead instead of them, if it hadn't been for the fire. 'Vengeance is mine, sayeth the Lord.' So. You suppose that's true?"

"I wanted to help get them," Clayton was appalled.

Juan said softly, "It seems to me I've heard about those murders. Your mother and the shooting of your father, that way."

"Yeah."

Otis observed, "Well, they sure got theirs. Hellfire couldn't've been any worse."

Jim commented, "You know, it was interesting. I have always wondered if I could help another man if there was really serious risk to myself. It's nice to know I could, but I do admit, I'm glad we didn't."

"Yeah." Clayton put a hand on Jim's shoulder. "I never would have let you. But I appreciate the fact that you would have backed me."

"You're welcome."

Otis looked at Juan. "Clay's a good man."

"I know that. What I worry about is what's ahead for him. He could really be hassled. You were lucky you weren't alone up there, Clay. You got these ones to vouch for you."

"Yeah. I appreciate it."

Jim said, "It was *his* parents, he did the right thing, and now he gets hassled. Strange world."

"He's got us," Otis comforted him.

After that, for Clayton, it was about like having two brothers. Jim and Otis stuck around him. Clayton was a loner. As he'd grown up he'd always longed for brothers, but if he'd been granted the choice of brothers, they wouldn't have been Otis and Jim.

They stood by Clayton and walked along with him, making him feel crowded. They watched out for him. And Clayton didn't know how to pry loose from their concern.

The rangers had immediately been to the scene of the accident and studied it initially from a fire-dictated distance. They'd noted the overrun barricade. They'd noted what was left of the black pickup, which was lying in odd, fire-shaped pieces there, and over there and all around in a large, stark, smoldering area. No one had escaped. The gas tank had blown. The fire storm had consumed almost everything. The rangers set a watch and the rest would return as the land cooled.

Then toward dawn, when the crew had been relieved and bused to the place where they would rest, the rangers came to interview the principals, which they tried to do discreetly. But the crew all felt they were a part of it. They were curious, and Otis was witness.

He made a good one. "Clay waved them to take the left fork. He had the orange flag. He yelled, 'No!' when they headed for the barricade, and you must have seen what they did to that. My pack's one of them that's busted. And Clay ran after them yelling, 'Stop!' I'll testify to that."

"So will I," Jim added soberly.

The head ranger said to Clayton, "You do know there'll have to be a hearing? We can't have anyone claiming you misdirected them in order to get revenge."

Otis said, "If they say that, they'll be admitting that those bastards killed his folks."

"Not necessarily," the ranger cautioned. "Only that he thought they did."

Clayton said, "They did. I saw their tracks."

And with curiosity, the head ranger questioned, "Why did you tell them to take the left fork, Clay? Did you recognize them?"

"Yeah. And they knew who I was. They tried to run the truck into me."

"Yeah," Otis and Jim agreed.

"They could have thought you were misdirecting them." One ranger put that in.

But another said, "No, they knew this country. They knew the left fork would bring them back to us. They had to get through, and they took the risk. Good riddance."

"But . . . I meant for them *not* to die." That was a troubling thought for Clayton and he still couldn't believe he'd tried to spare them.

The head ranger offered, "You're a Masterson. You're a good man. Good men do the things to protect and preserve."

"Protect and preserve? They were scum!" Clayton protested.

Otis said cheerfully, "Not anymore. In the ashes, you can't tell where they leave off and something else begins."

Jim observed philosophically, "They're nutrients for the flowers next spring."

"Stinging nettles," suggested one ranger who was familiar with the characters.

And there was agreement.

The rangers finally left. The members of the crew were all tired, but the dramatic experience kept them talking for a while.

Clayton longed for his fiddle, and the peace that its music could bring to his soul; but he wasn't sure where Shelley was stationed, and she still had the instrument.

After the meal, he took his blanket aside to sleep with nightmares, and must have cried out. He heard Otis tell him it was okay. And once he heard Jim's voice. He dreamed again and again of the encounter, and he heard his mother's voice. But her words weren't clear, and he strained to understand. She began to fade away, and he called to her as he struggled futilely to follow.

And Shelley appeared in his mind. She was solemn. He explained what had happened, and she turned her head to look at him. She was so beautiful to him that he quit speaking and just looked at her. And slowly he sank into deep and dreamless sleep.

When Clayton wakened early the next morning, Otis and Jim were watching him. He frowned.

"You okay, Clay?" Otis questioned softly.

"Yeah," he replied rather abruptly. "Why?"

Jim replied, "You were a little restless last night. Sounded as if you were fighting demons."

"That good-looking nurse Maggie was here fixing blisters," Otis explained. "She sat by you and put her hand on your head, and you quieted down finally."

"Maggie?" He was dismayed.

"You called her 'Shelley,'" Otis snorted with laughter.

"She didn't mind," Jim soothed. "She left her hand on your forehead and watched you."

"She's Dr. Johnson's." Clayton made that emphatic.

"Yeah. He was here, too. He said you were 'stressed,'" Otis added that.

Clayton was disgusted. Four people hovering over the Loner? How did he get a little breathing room? He—

"We brought you something to eat." Otis moved the piece of cardboard on which was a heaped breakfast plate. "Maggie said you're diet-deficient. There, Jim, did I get it right?"

"Perfect."

And Clayton's exasperation hit the intolerant mark. "I'm fine," he mentioned through clenched teeth.

"Have the coffee. That'll help," Jim said kindly.

"I thought Maggie said he was caffeined out?" Otis looked down his nose in disapproval.

Jim soothed, "He hasn't had any all night. We can't cut him off right away."

"I don't believe this." That had been a good expression on TV for quite a while.

"Eat," said Otis.

Since he couldn't think of anything that he could possibly say that wouldn't offend those two kind people, Clayton ate.

And Sam came over and hunkered down. "How's it going?" His tone was the one used with a rabid dog. It was gentle and cautious.

Clayton wondered what on earth he had done during the night that made everyone so careful of him. He gave Sam a glance and said, "Fine." But he remembered Sam teaching him to drive. And Otis and Jim had backed him. Then he thought with forbearance how fortunate he was to at last have friends.

But no one had ever mentioned that friends could be a pain in the neck. The good with the bad? He would learn to be tolerant. He might not like going back to being alone. He knew he needed Shelley. But he might also enjoy having the companionship of other people, too. This was a very odd position for a loner.

"What are you doing over at this place?" Clayton asked Sam. "Why aren't you with Spears?"

"I had some things to deliver here. I'm on my way back. Heard about the...incident. I'm proud of you, Clay." Sam reached out, clapped Clayton on his shoulder, then stood up and said, "I'll be around today."

Clayton ate, and friendly people came by and said things like, "Well, awake at last." and "Glad those rats got it," and "You shoulda told us about it. We coulda been looking for those guys."

Clayton nodded to acknowledge their overtures. But he also realized that his adopted "brothers" had made the whole meadow be quiet while he slept late.

Well, if a man was going to gather brothers, he would want ones who were prejudiced in his favor and who had clout. It looked as if he'd managed three of that kind. Otis, Jim and Sam. Sam was more amused by it all than Clayton. Maybe Clayton could learn that amused tolerance. His dad had always said that you can learn something from anyone you met. And Clayton wondered what he could learn from Otis?

They were allowed to be late getting started that day. The fires were moving, and it was very hectic. Everybody watched the clear smoke-free patches of the sky, which continued a brilliant blue. No rain in sight.

So they worked, and the time passed in stretches of tired muscles and dead sleep, so that "days" were a meaningless division. Only the kind of meals served punctuated the time. Like the meals, sleep time fluctuated. There were times when it was twenty-four hours of straight effort.

But the crews were fed good meals that were mostly hot. They begged for Popsicles...and Sam must have heard because he went into Jackson and brought back a full commercial-sized carton. The crews all went wild and looked strange because the icy treats were all blueberry, and their mouths were ringed in blue. One blue mouth would grin at another and comment, "So you know Sam," and the strange mouths would share a laugh.

The day that the stray wolf was mentioned the first time, Clayton didn't really pay attention. A lot of animals had been ousted from their natural places. But then someone said, "It had a yellow collar. It looks at all the people along the way, as if it's searching for someone."

"A yellow collar on a wolf?" Someone questioned that.

None of his crew had ever seen Wolf. Clayton interrupted bruskly, "Where was the wolf?"

"He's just around."

"Was he black?" Clayton tested the wolf's identity.

"No. Kind of mottled like most of the pictures you see."

Clayton was terse. "When did you hear this?"

"Today. Why?"

"He may be mine. Juan? I've got to leave. Something may have happened to Shelley. My wolf's loose."

Naturally Otis was within earshot. "Wolf? What's going on?"

"People are talking about a wolf with a yellow collar. My wolf was with Shelley. I've got to go."

"Where is this Shelley?" Juan asked carefully. "Show me on the map."

A chill went down Clayton. He walked carefully with Juan over to the map and pointed.

"I'm sorry." Juan told Clayton. "That's been overrun. If she was there, she'd now be here."

"She was one of the crew for this area." Clayton pointed on the map. "A first-aid and food dispenser."

"Then she would be there," Juan said. "Perhaps you would like to take my truck? Go and see."

"I need to go with him." Otis gave Juan a speaking stare.

Jim said, "I do, too."

"You can't both go," Juan protested. "I need every hand I can keep. Choose."

Clayton said a bit stridently, "I'm perfectly capable of driving myself over to the camp. I don't need anybody."

Jim was saying to Otis, "You go. I'll hold down the fort."

Clayton said in frustration, "Just lend me the truck."

Otis was firm. "We think you might need one of us, Clay. So I'm going. Adjust."

"Oh, hell."

Otis smiled. "That's the way."

Otis did try to talk, to distract Clayton who was tense and urgent in getting to Shelley. Finally Otis said, "All over, it's hectic. Don't worry. Wolf probably just got separated from her and he's looking for you. She's all right."

Clayton just made the sound: "Yeah."

"Don't borrow trouble."

"Just get me there."

"I'm doing that." Otis complained.

"Go faster."

"No." Otis was stubborn. "I want us there in one piece."

"I know."

Spears met them and said, "She must have evacuated. We've tried to call her, but the lines are down. She *was* warned."

"Did anyone see her after the evacuation?" Clayton asked harshly.

They found that no one knew anything about Shelley. Sam was there. He told Otis, "You go on back to your crew, I'll take care of Clay."

"But—"

Sam said, "I'm loose. I'll bring him back when I can."

Otis shook hands with Clayton and said, "Good luck. I'll keep an eye out for Wolf."

"Yeah. Thanks." Clayton wasn't used to help and he mostly forgot to express his appreciation. But now he was made aware of people helping him.

They drove toward Shelley's, but they were stopped by rangers. "Sorry, you can't go through."

"Do you know Shelley Adams? Did she get out?"

"I hope so."

"My God, man—" Sam was disgusted.

The ranger said, "Got a map?"

Sam got his out and spread it flat.

"Go to this place." The ranger pointed on the map. "They have a list of people who are displaced. It isn't accurate, but you might find out what you need to know."

Silently they drove there. But no one knew anything about Shelley.

"Sam, I need to go to the Loft. I need to get a ride and see. I have to."

"Let's go," Sam agreed.

At the Loft they were glad to see Clayton but hesitant over his request to see about a jump into that particular territory. And Sam took over. "Uh, could I have a word with your superior? He's an old friend."

"Who'll I say?" the man inquired dubiously.

"Sam Williams. We were in 'Nam together."

The guy smiled. "Sure. You were how old, ten?"

"I worked in the black market," Sam lied.

"You don't look Vietnamese."

He smiled an Irish smile. "All us Orientals are a mystery."

The scheduler laughed and went to a closed door, tapped, opened it and went inside.

One of the smoke jumpers inquired with a slight smile, "When were you in Vietnam?"

"That has nothing to do with it. Just about all men the commander's age who are still in government work were in 'Nam. Watch and see."

After a time the scheduler came out and said, "He's looking forward to becoming . . . reacquainted."

So Clayton was left with the man who scheduled the flights, and Clayton told him earnestly, "She's been working as a volunteer. She's given hours and hours and she's worth a flight by a DC-3. Please. Let me go look for her. And if she's trapped there, let me jump."

As the scheduler shook his head in a reluctant way, the door opened and the commander came out with Sam. The commander said, "I believe I should have an overview of what's going on. These men would like a ride. Will you see to it immediately?"

Ten

You know about the protective clothing?'' the guy who issued the gear inquired.

"Yes." Clayton was very serious.

"You can walk through a wall of fire with this, but the 'wall' can't be too wide. It isn't something to do carelessly. Your vision is limited by the helmet. You would have to be careful where you put your feet. If you tripped over a hidden snag or a log, and the covering is ripped, you'd be badly burned. And you could die right there. Understand?''

"Yes." Clayton didn't hurry the man. He listened attentively.

Sam watched.

"You know about the tents. I'm packing you two of 'em. If you have to go through actual fire, the outer one could be damaged. They don't last forever. Don't count on it—discard it. Understand?''

"Yes," Clayton replied.

"I checked this chute myself. I'd use it. You can trust me."

Gratefully Clayton said, "Thanks."

"Good luck."

They shook hands. Clayton put on the chute and checked out the smoke-jumper equipment he would have. He picked up the two supply rolls, and he said, "Now."

Sam and the commander went with him. No one said anything. They walked out to the Jeep and were driven out to the DC-3 that sat, motor throbbing, waiting for them. They got in, still silent. The plane was taxied to the runway, and they took off.

They flew until they came over the area of the fires, and they found the place where Shelley lived. That space of time took almost two hundred years in emotional time for Clayton.

The spotter said, "There we go. That's the place. Oh."

Fires blocked her house. The trees were burning vertically. The flames were clean. They could look down into the fires and see that the house still stood, and the pool was partly filled.

"She could be in the pool," said the spotter.

Clayton said, "Yes. I want to go in."

"You won't be able to drop into her pool or on her house. Your chute could go. You'll have to go down . . . there."

Clayton nodded. "Ask the pilot to make a couple of passes and let me look."

Sam and the commander watched and neither gave any advice or said a word.

The spotter asked, "You got the radio?"

"Yeah."

"If you can't go through, head for the south slope. You could last there."

"Yeah," Clayton replied.

"The fires are going outward. If you get to her, you will gradually be allowed more room as the fires go past. See? You know how to handle yourself once you hit the ground. Put on the helmet and take that bundle close against your chest. Got that?"

Clayton said again, "Yeah."

"What do you think? You know the terrain."

Clayton requested, "Ask him to come around from the south. I'll try for that place right to the east of the house. The fire's thinner there."

"Okay." The spotter talked into his head mike as the plane began another run.

Clayton readied himself. The spotter said, "Now."

And without another word, Clayton stepped out of the plane.

It never occurred to Clayton that he was doing something remarkable. His only thought was that he needed to get to Shelley. To jump was the only way. The updraft of the fires made his descent very difficult. He was jumping into a forest fire, hoping to land in an already burned area that wasn't very big. The alternative was to land outside the entire fire, and then getting to Shelley would be very hazardous. He could die trying. He would try.

Because he was so concentrated on doing what needed to be done, he did get down where he wanted to be. It was a miracle. He discarded the chute, put on the helmet and said, "I'm on my way," into the mouthpiece.

He began to walk through the least amount of fire that he could. He didn't become disoriented. He never lost sight of his landmarks and he watched closely, placing his booted feet carefully.

When he glimpsed the house through the flames, he was surprised it was that close. And he walked then, through the actual fire.

Taking careful, almost ponderous steps, he was aware that to fall now was death. He moved with extraordinary care, counting the seconds he had. And he made it through. There was the pool.

He moved as far as he could away from the fires. He finally reached the side of the pool and he saw her.

Into the radio he said, "She's alive." She was in the water, under the diving board. Her hair was wet, and her eyes were enormous. The pool was half empty.

He shed the helmet, the heavy boots and the extra shielding, but he carried the package with him. He walked down the clear steps and into the shallow end. He waded carefully through the water toward her, and she knew him. He saw her mouth open but she coughed and ducked again.

Then she came up and watched him, and he knew she was crying. He went to her and held her to him. He spread the probably damaged tent around her and over her head. He put the other ready if the fire should hit the house, and he held her.

He saw that there were other creatures taking refuge in the water. One was a snake. That gave Clayton some uneasiness. Shelley had apparently realized she would be joined in the pool, because she'd put boards, cushions and foam plastic into the water for creatures to mount. There was a rabbit, a skunk, the snake, two wood rats and a very distressed bobcat.

None of them moved after Clayton came into the pool. The bobcat hissed quite a bit, but no one challenged him.

And they survived. The house was scorched, but Shelley had put so much of the pool water on it that it had lasted. It was dry as a bone from the heat, and surfaces were warped and discolored. But it hadn't burned. Had it caught fire, they probably would have died.

There was cooler air drawn into the fire-vacated places. And they gasped. Clayton watched the snake that had become restless.

She whispered very huskily, "It bit a rat."

"It's nonpoisonous," he told her. "But the bites can be painful." He began to peel off his outer clothes very carefully, very slowly so that none of the creatures would become too alarmed, especially the skunk. He gave Shelley a soggy peppermint to suck.

Her eyes never left him and her hands were clutched around his waist. He held her up since he could stand in the depth of the water. The diving board overhead had helped her not be scorched. That and being in the water, which was heated by the fire to a depth of several feet down.

"Oh, Clayton," she finally whispered.

And he kissed her.

She began to shiver with nerves, and he held her tightly, steaming inside his protective clothing in that mostly warm water. He tried to get out of some more of the layers. She wouldn't let go, and that did delay him.

But he gave her more candy to suck. She drank a tube of the water and made a face. Her throat was irritated with the smoke she'd inhaled and her voice was husky as she whispered "Oh, Clayton" a great deal. And he finally got out of most of the layers and held her closely, wrapping her in the woolen shirt he'd worn, worrying that with the smoke irritation of her respiratory system, she would chill into pneumonia.

He asked her once, "Why didn't you leave?"

"I meant to. My car burned. Your fiddle is in the cave. I took it there."

And he asked grimly, "Why didn't you stay in the cave?"

"I thought I could save the house."

"Nothing is worth your life." His voice grated.

"How did you know to come to me?"

"Wolf was spotted away from you, and I knew he wouldn't leave you unless it was necessary to find me."

"Oh, Clayton."

"I'm here. You're okay. We're together. Here, drink this." It was a tube of fruit juice.

And after a long time, she said, "You looked like a knight, coming through that fire. That helmet—you were magnificent."

"I was scared for you."

"So was I. I love you, Clayton."

"Yeah."

"Say the words to me. I need them."

"You gotta know I love you," he said with some impatience. "I love you, Shelley. My life wouldn't be anything without you. I love you with all my heart. Why in hell didn't you get out of here?"

"This is not the time to get mad at me," she warned.

"I'd like to wring your damned neck."

"Clayton, I don't need this."

"You scared me spitless." He gritted his teeth. "I have every right to give you hell. You did a stupid thing, you damned near killed us both, and I'm feeling mad at you."

She watched him, and tears leaked from her open eyes all by themselves. "I guess you do have that right. I am sorry. But you can see that I did the right thing, and I would have been all right. You didn't have to risk your life getting here."

"But I love you." He almost snarled. "I'm going to take you to my cabin and nail up the door and get you thoroughly pregnant so you can't do anything but marry me and live with me forever."

"Are you proposing?"

"What's it sound like?" he asked in irritation.

"I think you could do a better job of it than that."

"If I get down on my knees, I'd drown."

She went back to: "Oh, Clayton."

"You're sure as hell a lot of trouble."

It was cooler. She put her arms out of the water, around his head and kissed him with all her heart.

He kissed her back and hugged her and held her and he said, "You're a damned nuisance."

And she laughed—a choking, coughing one.

It was some time before he left her under the diving board and emerged from the pool. The bobcat had vanished. The rats were hesitant. The rabbit and skunk stayed put. The snake had drowned.

Clayton examined the spray and wondered if it would work. He tried it, pumping with one foot, and he sprayed pool water around the pool, then flicked droplets over the house, and even from the pool, Shelley could see the droplets dance and sizzle.

He sprinkled the house quite a few times before he allowed the stream to fall on the parched, sizzling wood. But he finally wet it down again. The pump house was concrete, and it had survived. So had the pump. And he set it to refilling the pool. That would be a long, slow job, and there was an automatic shutoff.

He was sprinkling the burned ground between the house and the pool, when Shelley decided to emerge. She walked carefully. She was shivering almost uncontrollably. While Clayton was used to this proximity with fires, it was new to Shelley, and she was in a phase of shock.

He had to kick in the door before he could take her into the house. There were windows that had shattered in the heat, so the smoky air was moving in the house, and it was hot in there. The heat was good for Shelley. She stripped and found warm clothing and woolen socks.

Other than the exterior, the several windows and the smoke, there was no damage inside. Clayton took a sheet from the bed and carried it outside to lay it flat on the ground. It was a signal for a flyover that they were all right.

As Shelley warmed and calmed, she became rather sassy. "If I'd needed you," she said hoarsely, "I could have called. I was perfectly all right."

"You were glad to see me."

"I've always been glad to see you," she protested. "But you will notice that you really didn't need to lug all my things to the cave."

"You took down the fiddle."

"Well," she retorted. "You must admit, the heat and smoke could have damaged it. It needed to be in the cave. But the other things would have been perfectly all right . . . here."

"If I were you, I'd be very quiet and not call attention to myself. I'm in a chancy temper."

"Oh?" She put one hand on her hip, lifted her eyebrows and looked down her nose at him. "And just what do you think you can do about me?"

He regarded her stoically for a full minute, then he said softly, "I'll think of something."

He went out of her house and retrieved the equipment that he'd brought. He checked both of the fire shelters. He examined the suit and helmet of special material that he'd worn through the flames. All had survived. He secured them so that he could return them to the Loft.

The skunk and rabbit had left the pool, but Clayton didn't remove the floating objects in the water in case anything else needed a refuge. He went around the immediate area, patrolling. He watched and checked and paid close attention. The DC-3 flew over and Clayton stood on the sheet and held up his arm to only wave. The plane waggled its wings in response.

He continued to spray the house and the grounds close around the structure. Beyond that perimeter, the fires smoldered and the air was smoky and unpleasant to breathe.

Shelley called to him, and they ate. He told her, "When we can, we'll go to the cave. I believe we'd be better off there."

"All right."

He checked over her footwear and chose a pair of boots for her to wear. Just before dark, they took the trail to the south slope. It wasn't badly cluttered with debris because the trees had mostly stayed erect. Their needles were singed and some branches were bare. The forest looked like a mangy dog's back, but oddly there were patches of almost untouched portions bypassed by the rush of fires. The stranded pair could pick their way.

They went down the slope, along the still clear path. With the updraft, the air was cleaner to breathe. The cave was even better. They spread the rugs stored there and made a bed. They took off their clothing and lay together.

She nestled in his heat, but he was silent. She confessed honestly, "I'm glad that you came for me, I don't know what I would have done without you."

"You would've been okay," he assured her. "You'd done everything just right, except for the dumb thing of staying there. I came because I needed to be sure."

"I didn't know what to do next. I wouldn't have sprayed the house again. I wouldn't have thought to do that. And I wouldn't have come down here."

"You're having trouble breathing," he reminded her. "You'd have thought of the cave and that the things down here wouldn't smell of smoke. You'd have come down here without me."

"I'm glad you're here." She smiled sweetly.

"Me, too."

"I love you, Clayton."

"Do you?"

"Is there any question in your mind but that I do?"

"You told me not to come back unless I promised not to hunt those men." He felt her stiffen a bit. He told her, "They're dead." She gasped, and he admitted almost reluctantly, "I didn't kill them."

She was silent for a stunned while before she asked, "How did they die?"

So he told her about that shocking time. And he told her that he couldn't understand why he had tried to save them.

She said, "It's over. You're through with it. I'm proud of you. However it troubles you, Clayton, you did the right thing. Your conscience is clear."

He replied slowly, "I can't accept your relief because I don't know why I acted for them."

"It's over." She soothed him. "Let go of it. You are free of any responsibility."

"No."

She held him while he lay wakeful. But he didn't speak again nor did he move, and when she tried to cuddle with him, he didn't respond. She finally slept. And when morning came, they looked out on a white world. It had snowed in the night. Six inches of the early snow had ended the fires. The summer of fires was over.

They stayed in the cave for two days and the sun melted the snows. Clayton picked up his fiddle, turning it in his hands, but he didn't play it. He prowled the area and went to the house for food. She stayed in the cave or along the path. He didn't want her going to the house and breathing any more smoke.

He was silent and distanced. He couldn't shake his puzzling reaction to what had happened. He didn't understand why he felt this strange lethargy.

Shelley watched him. He didn't turn to her, his kisses were absentminded salutes and he didn't make love with her. Then she suggested, "Let's go see if your cabin is still there."

And he said, "Yes."

They tidied Shelley's blankets and rugs. After removing all the food that was still around, the pair went from the cave to her house. There, he chose the cloth-ing she would need for their trek, and they went down to the road.

They'd walked about three miles before a truck stopped to give them a lift. The driver exclaimed, "Clay! Well, this is luck. We were just talking about you, wondering what'd happened to you two. Sam will be relieved to hear you're okay. No one was worried, mind, but they just hadn't heard from you."

"Everybody okay?" Clayton wanted to know.

"Yeah. I think Otis and Jim left letters for you. They've gone on home."

Clayton asked, "Where are the letters?"

"At the Loft."

"I'll get them. Thanks."

The driver went out of his way to take them to Gasp. He said kindly, "Nice little town. You live here?"

"No. Our place is on beyond."

"Oh. Well. Good luck to you two."

"Thanks."

They went for coffee at the café. And Shelley sat eyeing the waitress. She leaned close to Clayton and whispered, "She the one?"

He looked around, then back to Shelley. "One . . . what?"

"You know. With the truck driver."

"Yeah." Clayton dismissed the fact.

"Really?" Shelley was amazed.

"Yeah."

"Oh."

They went to the general store and bought some tramping supplies to get them to his place. He didn't know how long it would take Shelley to walk it, so he counted on several days. He then had to buy a back-pack and a canvas and rope to rig a shelter.

Shelley was staunch. "I should help carry." And she gave him a look that would have made any stone respond.

He did look at her for a minute, but he didn't actually "see" her. He had to have understood her, for he got her a pack, too, and they started out.

His odd mood continued. He seemed introspective and a little morose. Shelley, too, became silent and thoughtful.

As they lay close but separately in the sleeping bag, she asked, "Are you still troubled by your reaction to the accident that killed those wicked men? You must realize that you have proven to yourself that you're truly a good man."

He reminded her, "I didn't deliberately signal them to take the left fork."

"That's what I mean. In spite of yourself, you instinctively did the right thing. I'm so proud of you."

"Don't be. I regret the law not getting them."

"No. I don't think so. I believe you regret that it's past. You were clinging to the hunt for those men so that you didn't have to think about the deaths of your parents. You could concentrate on finding the killers, and that way your parents were still with you. Now you have to let them go. That's why you feel so let down. You're grieving for them."

He was silent so long that she almost gave up. Then he asked softly, "Is that what this is?"

"I can't think of any other reason for you to be grieving. You most assuredly can't be sorry those men are dead. They were wicked."

And again he took a long time before he said, "You may be right."

But he didn't turn to her. He lay awake, silent and still.

The next morning as they made a small fire to boil water for coffee, he said, "I wonder what happened to Wolf."

"He would be all right, wouldn't he?"

"If he wasn't run over by some fool or shot by some Nervous Nellie."

"Are you being sexist?" She flung down a gauntlet.

He did hear that note in her challenge for he said, "Probably."

"With that admission, there's hope for you."

But he didn't respond to that.

It took a while, but he surprised her when he said, "You're being very patient with me, Shelley. I appreciate it."

"I wish you would let me in. I feel shut out from you."

He kissed her sweetly, but he didn't hug her. She thought maybe she should have stayed at her place until he'd sorted all this out. But he'd come to her in the fire. In her mind she saw him again in that medieval mock armor with an ersatz jousting helmet as he came through the fire to her. If he could do that, she could be patient with him now.

She looked ahead to Clayton as he led her farther from civilization. She realized he was a very basic man who was only just learning about the ramifications of being a civilized man.

His environment had dictated his basic reaction to the murder of his parents. If he'd been of any beginning culture, there would have been grieving songs and ceremonies to ease him.

But he'd been alone. No one had told him how to act. He'd never before known real grief. And he'd had to face the senseless murders of both parents, alone. He'd had no background in handling it, and he'd had no one to turn to.

He had her.

In the early afternoon, they passed the ranger in the fire-watch station and Clayton called, "Hello."

The ranger and his bitch dog came out on the walkway. The ranger leaned on the railing and called back. "Glad you're back. It's been lonesome up here all alone."

Clayton called, "Thanks for keeping an eye on things for me."

"You're welcome. Come by sometime."

"We will."

As the pair walked on, Clayton said to Shelley, "We've known each other for a while, but we haven't . . . visited."

"That must be a lonely post."

"Yeah. He carried his dog all the way up that ladder." And Clayton knew that he would become friends with the ranger. Clayton knew how to make friends now that he was no longer a loner. He turned and sure enough, the ranger was still out on the walkway, watching him. He lifted a friendly hand in farewell, and the ranger grinned and lifted his own hand in reply.

As the end of the second day approached, they came to a meadow. Clayton stopped and said to Shelley, "This is where our property begins. That's Masterson mountain."

She looked up the uneven, rather sprawled heights. "It's impressive."

"Beautiful."

"That, too." She agreed with him.

"Can you make it tonight?"

"I can do anything. Do you remember saying that to me?"

"It's true." He couldn't remember the incident.

She reminded him, "You said if I need anything to just call you."

"That's true, too. Do you need me to carry you up to my place?"

And she knew that if she asked, he would. "No. Not this time. Lead on, McDuff."

It was almost dark when they arrived at the cabin, still standing. They had known that it was still there or the ranger would have said something to warn them.

But there at the doorway was Wolf!

Clayton just laughed. So did the wolf. "So you got home! Come here, boy."

The wolf went to Clayton with his nose on the ground. Clayton knelt down and took the wolf in his arms, hugging him, ruffing his fur under his neck, freeing him from the yellow collar, talking to him. "No need to be sorry. See? I got your message. She's here. You don't have to be ashamed. You were successful. I heard. I went, and she didn't need me at all. But I appreciate all you did."

The wolf sat back and laughed at Clayton, appearing to understand all the words. Or was it just the approval?

Then Shelley held out her hand and the wolf was courteous. She said to Clayton, "He's back to being yours."

"Yeah. It's like the summer romances on TV—they always go back to their real place. Wait here. I'll get a light."

He went into the cabin and looked around. No one had been there. He frowned at the sprung spring on the sofa, then lighted a lamp and opened the door to Shelley. He looked at her standing outside, waiting.

Coming out again, he went to her and picked her up. "On TV the husband carries the wife over the threshold. I need to do that."

"Husband?"

He held her against his chest and looked down at her. "Yeah." He carried her very easily into the cabin. Wolf stayed outside. "You notice he understands he isn't supposed to be inside, here."

"But it's going to be cold tonight."

"Don't go ruining my wolf," Clayton scolded.

"I'll make him some sweet rolls tomorrow as a welcome home."

"Do I get some?"

"I'll have to see," she told him snootily.

"I have to go out to the root cellar for the mattress. The cellar isn't as good as your cave, but things do stay safe there."

She volunteered. "I'll help."

"Just hold the door."

It was quite cool and their breaths frosted in the air. Wolf pranced around, glad to see them. He watched Clayton carry in the stored things, and the mattress came in last. It was hefted up to the shallow loft on one side of the main room, over the door.

As if that was a signal, Wolf began to howl. Clayton and Shelley watched as the wolf moved around outside, doing that. It was as if he sang in gladness for Clayton's return.

But then weaving through the close howls of Wolf, there were distant ones that were...replying?

Wolf shot Clayton a grin and ran off into the darkness.

Clayton exclaimed, "Well, what do you know about that?"

"A lady?"

Clayton mused: "Did he watch us coming up here? He had to've heard us. Did he leave his lady and meet us here to say goodbye? I wonder."

She was silent as they sorted and tidied the returned objects.

So, too, was Clayton silent. He looked around at the rough cabin that his father had built and his mother had softened. He looked out over his father's land, knowing it had nurtured Mastersons for going on three hundred years. And he really understood that he was a part of a long succession of people. He wasn't a loner. He was a part of everybody. He looked at Shelley and knew that she, too, was a part of another line and that those lines merged in them. Once separate, they now made another whole. He'd never been a loner, he'd only been alone.

She surveyed the cabin. "Do you share my mattress?"

His heart melted to see her there. "Your mattress? That's mine, and you have to convince me that you get to sleep with me."

"How do I do that?"

With a smile, he remembered the phrase from TV, "You wing it."

And she laughed.

They had some cocoa with canned milk, and they had some of the food from their supplies. He showed her that he had a freezer and a smokehouse and was stocked for the winter. She inquired, "You're here for the winter?"

"Aren't you?"

"Well, I really don't have much with me." She confided. "I would need a few supplies."

"We can get anything we need in Gasp. Things like underwear and socks and a marriage license."

"Oh?"

"You do remember that I'm going to nail shut the door?"

"Oh." She raised her eyebrows.

"And I'm going to make love to you all winter."

"I see."

"Not yet, but you will. Shelley. I think you were right in figuring me out. I've spent these days thinking about my parents, and I know they are gone forever, in a way. In another way they'll always be a part of me. And that part I'd like to share with you. They gave me love and pride and responsibility. I can give those things to you."

"Oh, Clayton."

"Come to me."

And she did. She was kissed and loved and cuddled and soothed. He took off the impeding materials that so selfishly covered her, and he stripped away the things he wore that hampered their touching. And he took her to his bed in the crawl space of the loft.

He told her how beautiful she was and how much he loved her. Then he said how he liked to touch her and he showed he those ways. She was shocked, and demurred.

But he kissed her in a lot of squishily titillating ways and murmured incinerating suggestions, and she gasped and wiggled and helped. He was scandalized as he moved her hands the way he wanted them to go, making protestations all the while he was being outrageous. And she laughed.

Her body was heated and excited and she moved languorously, with insinuations. And he was hotter than a two-dollar pistol and tremblingly eager.

She touched and tickled and smoothed her hands on him, while he kneaded and rubbed and swirled his own on her. Then he took her hands and moved them more boldly on his body, and she became serious and her eyelids got very heavy, while her breaths panted.

His own breaths were scorching and quick. He became filmed by his passions, and he trembled like an aspen leaf in the stillness of summer.

When he took her, she clenched her teeth and knees and muscles and then stretched her body to touch all of his in a sinuous dance. And he felt her beneath him, around him, loving him, and he knew that she was all he needed. All he wanted. This perfect woman, whom he had recognized the first time he'd seen her, and known that she was his.

*   *   *   *   *

Double your reading pleasure this fall with two Award of Excellence titles written by two of your favorite authors.

Available in September

DUNCAN'S BRIDE
by Linda Howard
Silhouette Intimate Moments #349

Mail-order bride Madelyn Patterson was nothing like what Reese Duncan expected—and everything he needed.

Available in October

THE COWBOY'S LADY
by Debbie Macomber
Silhouette Special Edition #626

The Montana cowboy wanted a little lady at his beck and call—the "lady" in question saw things differently....

These titles have been selected to receive a special laurel—the Award of Excellence. Look for the distinctive emblem on the cover. It lets you know there's something truly wonderful inside!

DUN-1

Take 4 bestselling love stories FREE

Plus get a FREE surprise gift!

SILHOUETTE·INTIMATE·MOMENTS®

Premiering this month, a captivating new cover for Silhouette's most adventurous series!

Every month, Silhouette Intimate Moments sweeps you away with four dramatic love stories rich in passion. Silhouette Intimate Moments presents love at its most romantic, where life is exciting and dreams do come true.

Look for the new cover this month, wherever you buy Silhouette® books.

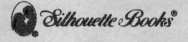

Silhouette Books®

Win 1 of 10 Romantic Vacations and Earn Valuable Travel Coupons Worth up to $1,000!

Inside every Harlequin or Silhouette book during September, October and November, you will find a PASSPORT TO ROMANCE that could take you around the world.

By sending us the official entry form available at your favorite retail store, you will automatically be entered in the PASSPORT TO ROMANCE sweepstakes, which could win you a star-studded London Show Tour, a Carribean Cruise, a fabulous tour of France, a sun-drenched visit to Hawaii, a Mediterranean Cruise or a wander through Britain's historical castles. The more entry forms you send in, the better your chances of winning!

In addition to your chances of winning a fabulous vacation for two, valuable travel discounts on hotels, cruises, car rentals and restaurants can be yours by submitting an offer certificate (available at retail stores) properly completed with proofs-of-purchase from any specially marked PASSPORT TO ROMANCE Harlequin® or Silhouette® book. The more proofs-of-purchase you collect, the higher the value of travel coupons received!

For details on your PASSPORT TO ROMANCE, look for information at your favorite retail store or send a self-addressed stamped envelope to:

PASSPORT TO ROMANCE
P.O. Box 621
Fort Erie, Ontario L2A 5X3

 ONE PROOF-OF-PURCHASE

3-CSD-1

To collect your free coupon booklet you must include the necessary number of proofs-of-purchase with a properly completed offer certificate available in retail stores or from the above address.

© 1990 Harlequin Enterprises Limited